D1094063

MAR   1997

WORST CASE

SCENARIO

WORST CASE

* * * * * * *

SCENARIO

a

washington, d.c.

mystery

★

michael bowen

crown publishers, inc.

new york

Copyright © 1996 by Michael Bowen

Published by Crown Publishers, Inc., 201 East 50th Street, New York, New York 10022. Member of the Crown Publishing Group.

Random House, Inc. New York, Toronto, London, Sydney, Auckland
http://www.randomhouse.com/

CROWN is a trademark of Crown Publishers, Inc.

Printed in the United States of America

Design by Karen Minster

Library of Congress Cataloging-in-Publication Data
is available upon request

ISBN 0-517-70149-9

10   9   8   7   6   5   4   3   2   1

First Edition

For CAB,

of uncommon understanding

★

WORST CASE
SCENARIO

autumn
1990

★

It's everywhere," the voice on the telephone said. "TV, newspaper, talk shows, beauty salons, and coffee shops."

"Lead story?" Jeffrey Quentin asked, fondling the birthday card, tracing with his thumbnail the Hummel-perfect little-girl drawing that graced its cover.

"Three columns wide on the front page. I haven't seen local headlines like this since a Wilmot High kid got a football scholarship to Ohio State. Two references to girls under sedation. Plus this morning I heard a rumor about a nervous breakdown."

"Local media on that rumor?"

"Not yet. I only heard it this morning."

"Well, get your ass in gear," Quentin said jovially. "I'll be there first thing tomorrow."

Richard Michaelson, for several good reasons, thought Deborah Moodie was a saint. For pretty much the same reasons, a number of other people in Washington thought she was a royal pain.

Scott Pilkington, for example.

Which was supposedly why Pilkington was in West Virginia, talking with Michaelson and Deborah's husband, Alex.

"Deborah's career has stalled," Alex Moodie said. "I need to find out why so that she can do something about it."

"I don't like being the bearer of bad news," said Pilkington, who rather enjoyed being the bearer of bad news, "but your wife's career hasn't just stalled. It has stopped. Permanently. And there's nothing she or anyone else can do about it."

"Deborah is a proud woman," Moodie said. His slightly rising voice was intense but still calm. Only the swizzle stick twisted spastically around his black fingers and his unconscious lean forward across the table suggested agitation. "But she's spent her life in government service and she knows how the game is played. If some super-grade needs more respect, she has lots of respect to offer. I just need to know." *Now*, his tone added.

Pilkington turned his attention to an unenthusiastic examination of his glass of wine. As he appraised it in the muted, late-morning sunshine that filtered through a skylight twenty floors up, his expression suggested that the second-rate libation was exactly the kind of thing you had to expect at an event like the Contemporary Policy Dynamics Conference and a place like the Charleston, West Virginia, Radisson.

"It's too far gone for that," he said then with what amounted to a verbal shrug. "The situation is irretrievable. Deborah Moodie has become the civil service equivalent of Kansas City: she's gone about as far as she can go."

"Why?" Moodie insisted.

"Woodstein syndrome," Pilkington said, without taking his eyes off the wine.

"What's that?" Moodie demanded, his voice sharpening.

"Amalgamation of Woodward and Bernstein," Pilkington said. "Kind of an obsession. Two unknown reporters uncover the biggest scandal since Teapot Dome and bring down a president. Overnight, every journalist in America decides that he's going to expose a head-grabbing scandal of his own. They don't have time to cover the zoning board meetings or the service club lunches anymore because they're all out looking for Deep Throat."

"Deborah is the deputy director of Planning and Research Priority Assessment with the National Health Research Agency," Alex Moodie said. "I don't see the connection."

"A few years ago the American Centers for Disease Control had its own Woodward and Bernstein. Her name was Elaine Thomas. She figured out that AIDS was a big deal before anybody else knew what it was, and she traced it to homosexual behavior when all the other experts were looking at street drugs and food additives. Just as all those eager young reporters wanted to be the next Woodstein, lots of people in public health want to be the next Elaine Thomas. Your wife seems to be one of them."

"What specifically are you referring to?"

"She thought she'd sniffed out a scandal. Some general getting a relative bumped way up the priority list for a rare-match liver transplant."

"And she was supposed to sit on that?" For the first time anger showed unmistakably in Moodie's voice.

"No. She was supposed to make a report in triplicate on eighty percent recycled paper, turn it over to the responsible office, and go back to assessing research priorities or prioritizing research assessments or whatever the taxpayers are paying her to do. But she got hung up on this favor-to-the-general business. She got her teeth into it and wouldn't let go. Obsessed. Hard to stay interested in mundane things like your job when you're tracking the public health scandal of the decade. Got to be downright annoying. So. She's plateaued out."

"At forty-nine?" Moodie demanded.

"Whatever age she is, she's going to retire as what she is right now."

Implacable certainty colored the flat, harsh words. The verdict was unappealable. Moodie looked jerkily away from the other two men at the table for a moment. He emptied his glass, without seeming to taste the contents.

"Had you heard this?" Moodie asked Michaelson when he looked back.

"The gist of it. But Mr. Pilkington feared it would lose something in the translation if he just gave me the story and let me pass it on to you. He declined to provide any details unless I arranged for him to bring you the message face-to-face."

"Why?" Moodie asked Pilkington.

"I understand you're still highly regarded at USIA," Pilkington said.

"I understand the same thing," Moodie said.

"Your interest in your wife's career is natural, and I can easily imagine your bafflement when the promotions suddenly stopped coming. I think it was quite shrewd of you to ask an old Foggy Bottom hand like Richard here to get on the telephone that the Brookings Institution so thoughtfully provides to him and start throwing metaphorical elbows into bureaucratic kidneys until he found the answer."

"But what?" Moodie prompted.

"But now that you have the answer, you wouldn't want anyone to think that you in your turn have become obsessed with something oblique to your own career responsibilities. The people in charge these days are long on process and short on imagination. Pursuing this might strike them as another example of Woodstein syndrome."

Pilkington leaned back in his chair. His suit, charcoal gray with a rich weave that announced four figures even at a casual glance, hung perfectly over a chunky, mid-forties frame. As he finished his wine, you could tell from the wistful look in his gray eyes that he was regretting the delicately nuanced bouquet of a recently sampled and far superior vintage.

"Well," he said, rising, "thank you for the drink and the opportunity to talk." The other two men stood as well and he shook hands with each of them. "Richard, I've delivered as promised, and I do eagerly request fifteen minutes of your time in exchange."

"A promise is a promise," Michaelson said, nodding. He and Moodie sank back into their chairs as Pilkington strode away.

"This was a thankless chore," Moodie said to Michaelson. "I know it was an imposition. I appreciate your digging the information up, even if it is bad news."

"I'm glad I was able to do it," Michaelson said. "No matter how bad the news is, it's better to know than not to know."

Left unspoken was why Michaelson had agreed to Alex Moodie's plea that he look into the reason for Deborah Moodie's sudden career blockage. He and Alex Moodie had been colleagues during Michaelson's years with the foreign service, covering the same geographic area for agencies that had to work closely together. That was part of it, but without the back-channel connection it probably wouldn't have been enough.

"Back channel," rich with cloak-and-dagger connotations, is really just shoptalk for a way to get information from a U.S. embassy abroad to Washington without telling the ambassador on the scene (or the deputy chief of mission, or the CIA station chief—it depends). Lots of radios, teletypes, and fax machines can be back channels. When Michaelson was active in the foreign service, many of those were controlled by the USIA. The catch was that a USIA officer had to look the other way (or not), and then tell curious folks like Michaelson what happened (or, perhaps, not tell them). Alex Moodie had had to make those decisions several times in cases that interested Michaelson, and in Michaelson's opinion he'd always gotten it right.

That was it. Nothing heroic, nothing all that special. Just doing his job, really. Just getting it right when it mattered.

Aggravation flickering through his brown eyes, Moodie glanced at Pilkington's retreating figure.

"He's never been at Near East/South Asia, I know that," Moodie said. "What's his area?"

"Pilkington has always preferred administration to hands-on diplomacy. For the last eight years he's been assigned to the State Department's Office of Intra-Departmental Inquiry."

Moodie looked up sharply at Michaelson.

"In other words," Michaelson said, catching the look, "he's a cop. And he's very good at what he does."

"Contemporary Policy Dynamics Conference" was a new title for the event, but everything else about it was pretty much the same as in previous years. People from Washington had come to West Virginia for this year's CPD, looking for the usual things.

Sharon Bedford was looking for a job.

Wendy Gardner was looking for money.

Alex Moodie was looking for information.

Scott Pilkington was looking for contacts.

And Jeffrey Quentin was looking for a piece of paper.

Literally: a single page of high-quality, watermarked bond paper about nine years old. He figured it would be worth millions.

Not millions of dollars. Millions of votes.

Michaelson caught up with Pilkington again thirty-five minutes later, at the registration desk. After picking his way through a crowd of Perrier-swilling, nicotine-deprived, mixed-gender CPD attendees who had spilled out of a first-floor Get

Acquainted Room, Michaelson finally managed to reach Pilkington's elbow.

"Is my room ready yet?" Pilkington asked a harried desk clerk. "When I registered an hour ago, they told me to check back around now."

"That's 'Pilkington,' " Michaelson said to the clerk in a trying-to-be-helpful voice. "P as in ponderous, I as in ithyphallic, L as in—"

"Now, now," Pilkington interrupted. "You're the one who went after the story. Bad form for Oedipus to blame Tiresias when he finally finds out it's been Mom in the sack all these years."

"You might have been a bit more sympathetic. Deborah Moodie started her public health career patching marines up at Da Nang. She is utterly dedicated. I've never heard her refer to her 'agency.' She calls it her 'service.' She's a gifted administrator with a genuine sense of mission, and on top of that, she's a fundamentally decent person."

"One key or two?" the desk clerk asked.

"Two," Pilkington said, glancing over his shoulder at the milling crowd. "Hope springs eternal."

The clerk put two hard plastic cards in a small folder and handed it to Pilkington.

"Now let's see," Pilkington said, turning around and resting his elbows on the desk. He surveyed the crowd with the practiced eye of a veteran conferee. "Jeffrey Quentin is to the right, so we shall reach the elevators by heading to the left. With no expectation of being up for ambassador anytime soon, I'd just as soon avoid him."

"I thought he was a presidential aide on the domestic policy adviser's staff," Michaelson said as he obediently fell into step behind Pilkington.

"Yesterday's news. Formal announcement on Monday. He's a freshly minted White House liaison for foreign policy."

"That's encouraging, I suppose," Michaelson said. "Now that we have a foreign policy liaison, maybe soon we'll have a foreign policy."

They reached the elevator and rode to the ninth floor. Michaelson had assumed that meeting him at the CPD was Pilkington's idea of hiding in plain sight. In Washington, their meeting for a late-morning drink with Alex Moodie followed by a private chat might have been noticed by some chance observer and could have set tongues wagging. Here, in the compressed microcosm of Washington that the CPD Conference represented, their encounter was inevitably spotted by dozens of people, and no one thought a thing about it.

Now that he was on the scene, however, Michaelson found himself less confident of that comfortable assumption. Jeffrey Quentin ordinarily wouldn't have walked across Constitution Avenue to attend a bloviation festival like this, much less flown to West Virginia. Neither would Pilkington, for that matter. A nasty little intuition nagged at the back of Michaelson's mind like an unwelcome red light glowing on the dashboard: Something was going on here. Something more than chin-wagging self-promotion. Something that was certainly important, probably unpleasant, perhaps ugly.

"Haffez Amahdi," Pilkington said as he entered his room, naming a onetime finance minister for a small but fabulously wealthy country near the Persian Gulf. "Early eighties. Ring a bell?"

Stopping at the edge of the entryway, Michaelson watched with detached interest as Pilkington strode across the room and threw himself into a low-backed chair near the window.

Streaming sunlight emphasized the contrast between Pilkington's thinning, white hair and his deeply tanned face. Now in the privacy of his room, he took brown horn-rimmed glasses from inside his suit coat and parked them precariously on the bridge of his nose.

"If you have access to the file," Michaelson said, "you know more about the Amahdi episode than I could possibly remember. If you don't have access to the file, I can't tell you a thing—as you know perfectly well."

"Lymphoma. Brought secretly to the United States for treatment. Kept here three weeks and then quietly returned, all without a peep in the press—which was a damn good thing, because one leak would've sparked embassy riots in at least four countries. With the cowboy we had in the White House at the time, just itching to send the Eighty-second Airborne somewhere or other, it might've gotten very interesting."

"You've seen the file," Michaelson acknowledged with a nod and a shrug. "The intelligence assessments were a bit alarmist, by the way. A lot of those predicted riots never happen."

"Only four Americans were in on the whole story, and one of them is dead. Someone's been popping off to the Fourth Estate about something that sounds a lot like this, and—"

"And I am arithmetically one-third of the suspects?"

Pilkington made a show of counting on his fingers and moving his lips as he did sums in his head.

"Thirty-three and one-third percent, that's correct," he said then.

"Not guilty."

"What a relief. You do understand the consequences?"

"No, I don't," Michaelson said. "When that incident took

place, the United States had lost its last war, it had just finished ransoming hostages from an Islamic country for the first time since Jefferson's administration, and the Soviet Union was a seemingly unshakable superpower. Things today have rather turned around. That little piece of diplomatic history you alluded to is about as relevant to Washington right now as the Battle of Actium."

"Process, Richard, process," Pilkington said, like a despairing Latin tutor whose student couldn't master the third declension. "The national pastime isn't baseball or football anymore, it's galloping paranoia. There's a morbid public obsession with government conspiracies, emphatically including medical conspiracies. Probably twenty million people in this country actually believe the AIDS virus was concocted by the CIA. Americans have been murdered in Guatemala over rumors about snatching children for organ transplants. Former French cabinet members are facing jail for letting AIDS-contaminated blood be used for hemophiliac transfusions. And so forth and so on and et bloody cetera. We already have a foreign policy that looks like a slow-motion train wreck. Pander to the ambient hysteria with another confected scandal and we can write off the next few years along with the last few."

"There must be a much higher premium on imagination at the fudge factory these days than there was before my retirement," Michaelson said, shaking his head. "But you can put your fevered mind at ease. I'm not telling tales to the scribblers, and I'm not going to."

"Well, I believe you, of course," Pilkington said. Coming from Pilkington, this conveyed something between studied agnosticism and utter disbelief.

"Glad to hear it," Michaelson said.

"I do wish I could come up with some plausible explanation for the journalistic sniffing about that's suddenly gotten so hot and heavy in this area. I don't have a very high opinion of the trade myself. I've always said that working for a daily newspaper must be like producing pornography without the redeeming element of sexual gratification."

"I think I have heard you commit that simile before, now that you mention it."

"But I assume reporters aren't complete morons and that they have something to go on when they start down a trail."

"Good luck," Michaelson said. "I wish I could help you, but I can't."

"Please do keep our little talk in mind, then," Pilkington said. "They can't go on like this, you know. The White House, I mean. Regardless of how the next election comes out. Sooner or later they simply have to make some real changes, get someone who knows a hawk from a handsaw into the game. It would be a shame for you to deal yourself out just when your card's about to turn up."

This was Michaelson's most vulnerable spot. In his early sixties, retired for several years from the foreign service, chafing under a sinecure at Brookings, passed over a number of times for senior policy-making positions that he coveted, Michaelson made no attempt to conceal either his ambition or his disappointment at its frustration.

"Congratulations on not mixing your metaphors," he said with cold gentility to Pilkington. "Have a pleasant afternoon."

He walked out of Pilkington's room morally certain that no reporter in America gave two rips about secret medical treatment given to a rich Arab politician more than a decade ago.

Pilkington's real worry was something else related in some conceptual way—some covert governmental action with foreign policy implications and involving medical care. How had he put it? "Something that sounds a lot like this."

Whatever it was, he thought Michaelson knew something about it. Why did he think that? Because Michaelson had looked rather aggressively into Deborah Moodie's problem? Maybe. Michaelson's real reason for doing that wouldn't make sense to Pilkington, who'd assume that Michaelson was pursuing some personal agenda. Pilkington wanted Michaelson to earn the bribe (or avoid the threat) implicit in his heavy-handed sermon by telling what he knew. He expected Michaelson to clear himself of suspicion by saying *No, silly, those reporters aren't after the Amahdi story, they're looking into something else altogether. Now listen carefully.*

That much was reasonably clear. Less apparent was why Pilkington had gone out of his way to let Michaelson know that Jeffrey Quentin was here. That Jeffrey Quentin had suddenly acquired a foreign policy title. And that Pilkington didn't like Jeffrey Quentin. That Pilkington wanted Michaelson to reveal something was obvious. What Michaelson couldn't figure out was why he wanted Michaelson to disclose it to Jeffrey Quentin instead of to Pilkington himself.

How do you square your criticism of administration policy with your support of U.S. forces deployed pursuant to that very policy?"

"Once American troops are on the ground," Wendy Gardner said, "ties go to the president."

All right, she thought as she rose from her seat on the dais and shook hands with the five other hopefuls who'd shared it with her, so it isn't Edmund Burke. These aren't the sheriffs of Bristol, either. And don't forget, Burke *lost* that election.

She didn't intend to lose hers. That was why she was here, auditioning for people who controlled soft money and rich contributors and party resources that could make the difference in a tight race. That was why she'd asked Michaelson to come, to lend the heft of his foreign service reputation and Brookings affiliation to the credentials of a candidate barely over the minimum constitutional age for the office she was seeking.

Among other things, the CPD Conference was a cattle call, open casting, pick your metaphor. Show time for wannabes who thought they could knock off an opposition incumbent or, like Wendy, outrun an anointed heir apparent for an open seat. Sort of a low-rent, legislative-branch version of the famous Renaissance Weekend in North Carolina, but scruffier, dispensing with intellectual pretension, pure politics.

Wendy made her way through the milling crowd, offering eye contact and a smiling nod in response to murmured compliments, some perfunctory and some with real meaning. Then, as she reached the last row of seats, a woman approached her more aggressively.

"That was great," she said, reaching out and tentatively touching Wendy's arm. "You give good sound bite."

"Thank you."

"I'm Sharon Bedford. I sent you my résumé a few weeks ago. I was hoping to meet you here this weekend, so I brought another copy."

"I appreciate that," Wendy said. She glanced at the two proffered pages long enough to see National Security Council staff, then slipped them into a thin briefcase she was carrying. "I *will* look at this the minute I have time. I know how important good staffers are, and I make all staffing decisions myself. It's months away and miles to go, but if I win, I'm going to want to hit the ground running."

"That's actually something I was hoping to talk to you about if you could give me two minutes," Bedford said. Her eyes shone with quiet intensity, and a tone of controlled urgency colored her voice. "I know you need to blitz the hospitality suites and network some more, but if you were planning on hearing Dr. Marciniak, he's in this room in less than twenty minutes. We could talk here a little while we wait."

Wendy checked her initial impulse to brush Bedford off. For one thing, Bedford was right: Wendy had circled Marciniak's presentation on her program, and in the few minutes before it began she couldn't see running around like a sorority pledge during rush week.

On top of that, Wendy found Bedford's eagerness engaging. Wendy knew how hard it was for Bedford to walk up to her cold, risking a coffin-plate smile and a world-class blow-off. The CPD was brimming with twenty-three-year-old cynics, precocious Washington veterans with hard eyes and downy cheeks. Bedford wasn't one of them. Whatever Bedford was after, she really wanted it and she wasn't afraid to show how important to her it was.

"Sure," Wendy said. "Let's talk."

They sat down in the back row.

Bedford looked like she was in her early thirties. She had striking chestnut hair, somewhat curly, as if it had been permed, say, a month ago. She was within an inch or so of Wendy's height. In California she'd have been ten pounds overweight, but she'd be just about right in the Midwest, where boys like their girls with a little meat on their bones. Her nails were short and uncolored, and Wendy suspected that she spent a lot of time at a keyboard. Her manner suggested someone who planned things carefully. Wendy would have bet, for example, that she'd spent forty minutes in front of the mirror deciding what she'd wear today.

"Two things," Bedford said. "First, I guess I think what looks like a weakness on my résumé is really a strength."

"Would you like to explain that?" Wendy asked.

"The job changes, the instability. After I left the National Security Council staff—"

"Did you quit or were you fired?"

"Oh, I was fired," Bedford said, her tone suggesting surprise

15

at the notion of leaving the NSC staff any other way. "Change of administrations, new guys come in, vertical stroke."

"Sure. I'm sorry, I interrupted you. You were saying after you left the staff."

"Right. I had two jobs where I lasted a little over a year. They were good jobs, too, and I knew I should've been grateful for them. It was just that neither of them could give me the kind of feeling I had about the NSC."

"Do you think sorting constituent mail and troubleshooting lost Social Security checks could measure up to the White House basement?"

"Yes. I was an administrative aide at the NSC. Glorified clerk. It wasn't that I was doing anything all that challenging. It's just that I was part of something that mattered, and I want to be again."

"I want the same thing," Wendy said. She smiled encouragingly, found herself pleased when this coaxed a blushing smile from Bedford. "You said there were two things. What's the second?"

"Are you a baseball fan?"

"I'm running for office in the Midwest. I have to be."

"You know what they always say about those muscular outfielders that the contenders trade for in June? 'He can help the team right away'?"

"Sure," Wendy said.

"That's what I can do. I can get you some serious face-time. Separate you from the crowd. I can give you something that'll get the attention of the right people at the right time."

I have a trump card, Wendy translated mentally, *and I want this job enough to play it.* The tease was blatant enough, but Wendy couldn't ignore it. Roughly a hundred million Americans would like to be in Congress, and only five hundred and thirty-five of them can be.

"If you have something that hot, shouldn't you trade it for something more exalted than the staff of a potential House freshman?"

The question was a test and Bedford passed.

"I won't lie to you," she said. "I'd like an offer closer to a real power center, and if I get one I'll take it. But I give you my word: if you say yes first, the auction's over and your bid wins."

"Could you be a little more specific about what I'm bidding for?" Wendy asked.

"Not here. But maybe later, if you're interested after you've thought it over? I'm in the room on the second floor next to the political software company's hospitality suite."

"Okay," Wendy said. "I'll give it some thought and I'll try to stop by. But if I can't, don't hesitate to follow up."

"Don't worry," Bedford said, her smile now broad and warm, "I'm not the least bit shy."

A stone-faced, shiny-headed man introduced Jerry Marciniak, M.D., Ph.D., known to Beltway initiates as Dr. Marc. The stone-face reminded the audience, quite unnecessarily, that Marciniak was both a doctor of medicine and a research scientist holding a doctorate in cellular biology. He had served in an array of obscure public health outposts, including a stint in the late eighties and early nineties as director of the National Medical Records Compilation, Data Collection and Privacy Concerns Bureau, which he often said was every bit as exciting as its name suggested. He'd gone on to become assistant chief of the applied research staff at the National Institutes of Health and then, quickly and unexpectedly, had moved up to head the policy and planning directorate at the National Health Research Agency.

Wendy wasn't sure what she was expecting, based on that introduction. Marcus Welby in a lab coat maybe. Whatever it was, she didn't get it. Marciniak strode in wearing a kelly green cardigan sweater over a plaid shirt and khaki slacks. He took off a New York Mets baseball cap as he turned to face the audience and, seeing no place convenient to put the headgear, hung it by its adjustment strap from the microphone post. A spare six feet with Brillo-colored hair, he looked the audience over with lively green eyes before he launched into his talk.

Along with most of the people in the well-filled room, Wendy assumed he was going to talk about health-care reform: the eight-hundred-pound gorilla that no politician could ignore, the delicate question of having the government take over a piece of the economy ten times larger than the automobile industry without raising anybody's taxes.

She was wrong. He had come to talk about politics and science. Dr. Marc was here to preach the gospel. He spoke in a fast, catchy New York City dialect, his voice just this side of gravelly, referring to the audience as "boys and girls" with a smile and wink that made it all right. But he spoke with prophetic passion, and as he hammered the passages out, his eyes gleamed with Pentecostal flame.

Politics corrupted science. Politics had been corrupting science since before some impatient soldier cut Archimedes' throat, and it hadn't stopped. Labs and basic research outfits published articles every year based on data faked fourteen ways from Sunday. When the universities weren't cranking out cheap, Madison Avenue publicity for experiments that turned out not to be replicable, they were getting nailed right, left, and sideways for lying about what they were doing with grant money. And the nonacademic public sector was the worst of all. When AIDS was threatening the United States with its first fatal pandemic since the influenza scourge just after World War I, "our *best* scientists spent five *blessed* years arguing about who gets credit for isolating the virus."

Brief pause. Disgusted, cap-shaking slap at the podium.

"Science isn't about getting credit for isolating a virus," he boomed then. "Science is about finding a way to kill the damn thing."

Punctuated with a fist slam. Applause, scattered but enthusiastic. Some of the boys and girls were buying it. Wendy wasn't ready to swallow his argument whole, but Marciniak's sense of absolute conviction stirred her. In a weekend strewn with people who believed in nothing, she'd stumbled on a man who believed in something.

Why was this happening? Marciniak continued. The politics of money. The politics of greed. The politics of the golden rule: he who has the gold makes the rules.

Are things getting better? No, things are getting worse. Every day they get worse faster than they did the day before. We're not talking arithmetically, he insisted, we're not talking geometrically, we're talking exponentially. We have to find an answer. We have to protect science, insulate it from pressure groups, special interests, venal politicians.

There is absolutely nothing inevitable about progress, he concluded solemnly, nothing inevitable about the triumph of knowledge or reason or truth. The seventh century was a lot worse than the fourth, not a lot better, and at the end of the day the twenty-first might be just that much worse than the nineteenth. The choice was stark and simple: sweat now or bleed later.

Questions? No, no one had any questions. (If they asked questions, he might answer them.) The crowd gave him a respectable hand, then bolted for the door.

"He believes what he says," Wendy heard someone say on the way out of the room.

"Yeah," the stone-face who'd introduced him answered. "Thank God he's not in charge of anything important."

chapter

3

★

The Piaget watch the woman was wearing said 6:10, which meant that Scott Pilkington had fifteen minutes to get moving. The watch was the only thing the woman was wearing, though, and Pilkington knew he was in for a moral struggle. Concupiscence versus duty. He sighed at the prospect.

Carmen highlights wafted valiantly from the tiny speakers on the boom box/CD player Pilkington had brought with him. The woman—Katy? Sally? Kalli, that was it, Kalli Stern—was flipping through the other dozen or so CDs in Pilkington's attaché case.

"I never met anyone before who takes his own sound system along on trips," she said. "Once most of us get twenty miles outside Washington, it's tube all the way. CNN or C-Span, take your pick. I'm the same way."

"If you don't know it before it's on CNN," Pilkington murmured, "you might as well be a lawyer in Milwaukee."

Eyes closed for just a moment, he savored the *mot*, which he thought rather good. He decided to use it again sometime. Then he allowed himself another undisciplined glance at Kalli. Concupiscence was going to win.

"You got any Andrew Lloyd Webber?" she asked. "Sondheim, maybe?"

Jesus. Had we really turned the country over to people who found *Bizet* inaccessible?

"I think *Madama Butterfly*'s in there somewhere."

"That Sondheim?"

"Yes. Just before he changed his name from Puccini."

Rolling up to sit on the side of the bed, Pilkington began searching for his clothes. An upset victory for duty.

Kalli snapped her head toward him, her expression questioning and surprised.

"Sorry," he said as he pulled on a sock. "I have to see a woman."

"What am I, chopped liver?"

"No, darling, if you were chopped liver, you'd have better taste."

"Asshole," she snapped.

"You say that as if it were a negative thing."

Snatching at panties and bra, Ms. Kalli Stern stomped toward the bathroom, demonstrating in the process the singular aptness of her name. Pilkington sighed again. And found his other sock.

For a surreally exhilarating moment, on the strength of no particular evidence, Michaelson thought that the approaching woman wanted to seduce him. As she introduced herself, he realized with a mixture of relief and letdown that she only wanted to use him.

The relief didn't surprise him, but the letdown did. He wondered how he'd have dealt with an attempted pickup if one had been in prospect. *Sorry, I have an understanding with a lady in Washington?* As if he and Marjorie had worked out a fishing rights treaty with an odd codicil addressing this situation. He supposed so. He smiled at himself, reflecting briefly on the perils of being decades out of practice.

"I'm Sharon Bedford," the woman said, extending her hand.

Laying an open volume of Emily Dickinson's poetry facedown beside him on the weathered wooden bench, Michaelson rose and shook hands as he spoke his own name. With a gesture he invited her to sit next to him. They were on a quiet patio on the west side of the hotel, where strategically placed foliage and unobtrusive architecture provided the illusion of a tranquil rural view.

"I know who you are, actually," Bedford said. She tugged awkwardly at the hem of her skirt as she sat down. "I was on the NSC staff the first time you were up for national security adviser, not long after you retired from the State Department."

Bedford gazed at him in silence for a moment. He was over six feet tall, thin and angular. White-haired, with a look of politely detached interest in eyes so dark they seemed black. Half the pinkie on his right hand was missing—the result, Bedford knew, of collision with a ricocheting bullet during an embassy disturbance many years before.

"I wouldn't have thought of you as the poetry-reading type," she said, glancing at the volume he'd set beside him.

"For a long time I wasn't," he said. "I only got back to it last year, when I realized that I hadn't read poetry except in the line of duty in four decades."

"Line of duty?" she asked.

"Yes. Quite bad poetry, as a general rule, written by some potentate or minister I was trying to understand."

She didn't seem to expect further explanation, and Michaelson wasn't sure he could have provided it if she had. He'd enjoyed verse when he was twenty, as most educated people at the time did. For decades since, though, he'd treated good poetry like a well-crafted but never-used pair of cuff links that had somehow been shoved in the back of a drawer and forgotten. Mislaid, perhaps, as other important things had been during his working life.

Almost impulsively, he'd decided in his sixties to start reading poetry again. He'd done this simply for pleasure, filling idle hours and rediscovering a youthful enthusiasm. As he'd plunged more avidly into the thin volumes, though, he'd found himself reading his own perspectives into the verses and stanzas. It reminded him of a standard diplomatic history exercise in which dispatches about the same conference or the same negotiation by legates from the different countries involved are compared. It had occurred to him somewhere around the middle of a Dickinson poem that poetry and history were like that—accounts of the same human events by different legates from different countries. Or different worlds.

Tilting her head back slightly, Bedford let the evening breeze cool her face and neck. She shifted a cellophane pack of Hershey kisses from her lap to the bench beside her.

"You're here with Wendy Gardner, aren't you?" she asked then.

"Basically." An evasion, not a lie. "She's asked me for advice from time to time, and I'm vain enough to find that flattering."

"I'm trying to get a job from her. If she's elected. That's why I rode a bus for almost eight hours, pleaded with someone I'm not crazy about just to get a room here when the hotel was supposed to be sold out, maxed out on my Visa to stay at this place for two full nights. I want that kind of a job, and I'd do anything to get it."

Michaelson paused for a moment as she finished. The pause was long enough for her to read his expression and react to it.

"Bad girl, Sharon," she said, giving her left wrist a mocking swat with her right hand. "I overstated that, didn't I? I wouldn't be qualified for the kind of job I want unless there were some things I *wouldn't* do to get it."

"Understanding that much puts you well ahead of most of the people going after jobs like that," Michaelson said. "I know what you're talking about, and I don't blame you for feeling the way you do about it. At the same time, getting what you want might prove even more disappointing than doing without it. I was bitterly downcast a few years back when the new administration passed me over. Then, as I watched that administration limp from one fiasco to another, I realized that being ignored might have been the luckiest break I'd gotten in years."

"Maybe you could have made the difference between fiascoes and quiet, well-managed successes."

"I'd love to believe that," Michaelson said, "but realistically I don't think I could prove it. The people who were hired in place of me are very sound. Smart, tough, principled. The problem isn't those people. The problem is elsewhere."

"Maybe," Bedford said dubiously. "Even knowing all of

that, though, if the president called and asked you to be national security adviser, you'd take it, wouldn't you?"

"In a heartbeat," Michaelson admitted, smiling in recognition at the triumphantly grinning young woman.

"So you can understand how important the kind of job I want is to me."

"I can and I do. But I don't know how I can help. Ms. Gardner asks for my advice about foreign policy, not personnel decisions. If I lobbied her to put you on her staff, I'd do you a lot more harm than good."

"There's one way you can help," Bedford said. "I had a few minutes with Ms. Gardner this afternoon. I told her I could help her make a splash in a hurry. We didn't get into it in detail, but I think she was interested."

"I should think she would be."

"What I was talking about is in the area where she does take your advice. I'd like to go into it in depth with you."

"No time like the present."

She glanced at her watch, and Michaelson reflexively looked at his as well. Six-twenty. She handed him a piece of hotel stationery with a Bethesda, Maryland, address and a 301 area code telephone number written on it.

"I'm supposed to meet someone in a few minutes," she said, "and you're going to want to see what I'm talking about anyway instead of just having me tell you about it. If you're interested, I'd appreciate it if you'd give me a call sometime next week."

He was interested all right. This little chat was apparently just supposed to show him the bait. A call from him next week would tell Bedford how intrigued he was. If nothing better than a Wendy Gardner staff job was in prospect, she could

follow up; if someone at the other end of Pennsylvania Avenue had bitten, she could brush him off. If you have the
goods, you don't have to worry about finesse.

Michaelson just resisted the urge to seize Bedford's hand.
It wasn't just lack of finesse. Her innocence almost took his
breath away. In her early thirties from the look of her, Michaelson thought, Sharon Bedford was more naive than Wendy
Gardner had been at nineteen, when Wendy and Michaelson
had first met.

"How many people have you made this pitch to?" he asked,
trying to keep any suggestion of misgiving out of his voice.

"How many people are there here who could get me the
kind of job I'm looking for?" she asked as she stood up.

"There are two ways you can get in trouble in Washington," Michaelson said. "One is by promising what you can't
deliver. And the other is by delivering the kind of thing you
just promised."

"I know," Bedford said.

But Michaelson sensed with leaden certainty that she didn't
know. Not really. The inside of his belly suddenly felt cold.

"Now, *that's* craftsmanship," Jeffrey Quentin informed the
mirror as a talk-radio host reduced a dissenting caller to tinny,
impotent rage in the background. "That's a pro at work."

His intense blue eyes shining with fierce enthusiasm,
Quentin stared at the mess he was making of the knot in his
tie. His dark brown hair framed a round face that no one could
ever think of as threatening until their access was cut off or
their funding went out the window.

If JQ brought this one off, Quentin thought, it'd give those talk-show guys something to yammer about all right. He'd stage a campaign that Lee Atwater and Larry O'Brien combined couldn't have dreamed of. He'd be playing at the big table until they shut the game down.

Quentin checked his beeper, slipped into his jacket, took a last look to be sure the jacket matched his pants, and headed for the door.

chapter

4

★

The computer screen filled with dazzling blues, reds, and greens. A three-dimensional pie chart materialized. Polis Systems was about seven minutes into a heavy-duty software demonstration.

Sally Field, thought Wendy, whose attention was elsewhere.

She picked up only random snatches of the continuing patter: "... point and click ... sixteen-plus percent of ninety-eight forecast GDP ... any conceptual health-care plan now in play. . . ." Her focus was on Sharon Bedford, who was deep in conversation with a short, curly-haired man who Wendy finally realized was Jeffrey Quentin. Presumably because they were smoking, Bedford and Quentin stood well away from everyone else, isolated near a narrow, vertical window that had been cranked open to the maximum four inches that its security-conscious design allowed.

"Not impressed?" Jerry Marciniak asked Wendy from a few feet away, nodding toward the Polis presentation. "Health care's going to be the iceberg issue for the rest of your generation. Paying for medical services isn't just huge in itself, the cost is so enormous that it's going to have an effect below the surface on everything else. Within ten years you won't be able to talk about highways or weapons systems or anything else in Washington without looking at health care and its budget."

"The software they're peddling goes a lot farther than that," Wendy replied. "Those projections say that by the time I'm fifty the entire private sector will consist of health-care workers and insurance companies. I don't think that's going to happen."

Marciniak grinned. He was still wearing the outfit he'd had on when he'd given his speech that afternoon.

"I don't think it's going to go quite that far either," he said. "But we are spending money hand over fist on medical services. Every year we're spending more of it and spending it faster, and that's not gonna go on forever either. The only way to stop the cash hemorrhage is to build a wall for people to crash into when they're running away from death. 'No dialysis for you—you're too old.' 'No transplant for you—taxes are high enough.' 'No chemo for you—you're a goner in six years anyway.' "

"I think we'll do better than that," Wendy said.

"Data?" Marciniak challenged.

"None," she admitted, shrugging. "I just think we'll muddle through somehow until we stumble into some kind of messy compromise that halfway works most of the time. Americans are pragmatists."

"You're right," Marciniak said, "but we're the worst kind of pragmatists." Closing his eyes and pressing the fingers of his right hand together, he groped for a word. "We're *utopian* pragmatists. The bottom line for us is a new Jerusalem. Anything short of that is a Problem with a capital P—and like good little pragmatists, when we see a Problem, we want it solved before lunch by God, without a lot of chat about principles in the meantime."

"It does make for a sloppy kind of politics," Wendy acknowledged, nodding. "Of course," she added slyly, "you made your opinion of politics pretty clear this afternoon."

Marciniak offered her a biting smile.

"People ask me how I feel about politics, I ask them how Ed Norton felt about sewage," he said. "I spend my life up to my eyebrows in it, but how can I complain? Shoveling it up and making it flow is what I get paid for."

" 'It smells like money to me,' " Wendy offered, quoting a line favored by her state's paper mill owners when they found themselves downwind of a sulphur vat.

"Exactly. Let me give you one tiny example." Marciniak's voice rose in excitement as he warmed to the topic. "You know who's paying for this hospitality suite?"

"Polis Software better be paying for it," Wendy said. "They have their name on the door and they're hustling everyone who walks in here."

"I'm paying for the room. Or my agency is."

"Why?"

"Because three months ago when this thing was getting planned, I knew I'd have at least eight thousand dollars for travel, meetings and public appearances left in my budget, but I'd be running short on discretionary funds. So I called Polis and we swung a deal. I got a bunch of rooms including the suite, and I'm letting them use it. They'll reimburse the agency dollar for dollar—and that reimbursement will magically change my money from a categorical appropriation into discretionary funds."

"Our tax dollars at work," Wendy said mordantly.

"Totally legal. An absolutely one-hundred-percent legal scam that serves the public interest. Because there's no way that money wasn't going to be spent. We couldn't turn it back in to the Treasury without getting our next year's appropriation cut."

"I know."

"So if the end of the fiscal year was sneaking up on us with that money in the till yet, I'd have had to come up with a conference in Vancouver or someplace that we couldn't live without. This way, the money actually gets spent doing what my agency was set up to do."

"You really love this whole political mosh pit, don't you?" Wendy asked suddenly, intrigued by the epiphany. "You dump all over it, but you couldn't do without it."

"You got me," Marciniak said, smiling as he fixed a penetrating gaze on Wendy. "You read me like an X ray. And unless I miss my bet, you need it as much as I do."

"Everyone in this room does," Wendy said. "Look at Sharon Bedford, that woman over there in the corner pretending to smoke just so she can chat someone up."

"The one talking with Jeffrey Quentin?"

"Right."

"It doesn't look like she's pretending to me. I don't think there's anyone left anymore who smokes just to be polite. You're either addicted or you abstain. I'd put her and Quentin both in the addicted category—chronic self-mutilators."

"Look more closely. She reminds me of Sally Field in *Absence of Malice*."

"I don't catch many flicks," Marciniak said.

"Sally Field was supposedly this tough-as-nails reporter who was having trouble giving up smoking. Whenever she took a puff on the screen, though, she didn't look like she was having trouble stopping—she looked like she was having trouble starting. What she tried to pass off as smoking would've gotten her laughed out of the girls' lav at any self-respecting high school in the country. Same thing with Sharon Bedford. She's holding a lighted cigarette, but she's not really smoking. She's posing."

Marciniak studied the scene for perhaps ten seconds. The way Bedford held the cigarette did seem unpracticed, as if it weren't something she did habitually. Something studied and fastidious distorted the gestures she made with it, and while the drags she occasionally took looked technically competent, she didn't seem to approach them with unbridled enthusiasm.

"I don't think so," he said, frowning and shaking his head. "I'd say she's just very nervous, like someone who thinks she's out of her league all of a sudden. She'd probably look just as awkward to us right now if we were watching her eat or sew or something like that. Take my word for it: veteran addict."

"The guy she's talking to is someone who could get her a job on the inside again, isn't he?"

"Quentin?" Marciniak asked. "You bet he could."

"I'll bet you a bagel against a PAC top-contributor list that the only reason she's smoking is to give her an excuse to spend ten minutes alone with him."

"You're on."

Wendy waited until the Bedford/Quentin conference broke up and Bedford had begun to make her way across the room. Then Wendy moved unobtrusively to intercept the somewhat older woman.

"Oh, hi," Bedford said after a moment's surprise when she noticed Wendy.

"Hello again," Wendy said. "You know Dr. Marciniak?"

"Sure do," Bedford said, shaking hands with him.

"Nice seeing you again," he said, pumping her hand firmly instead of giving her a perfunctory, two-finger squeeze.

"I stopped you because there are no photographers around and I'm feeling existentially wicked," Wendy said then in a conspiratorial tone. "Can I bum a cigarette?"

Bedford looked stricken.

"I'd love to give you one but I don't have any," she said. In an almost comical anxiety to prove her statement, she opened her purse and displayed the tobacco-free inside to Wendy. "I just took one from Jeffrey Quentin, but I haven't actually smoked regularly since college."

"That's a lucky break, then," Wendy said, eager to reassure Bedford. "You've saved me from my first lapse in five years."

Bedford moved away, apparently warmed by Wendy's parting smile. Marciniak looked disbelievingly after her, opening his mouth once and then closing it tightly and giving his head one last puzzled shake.

"I owe you a bagel," he said quietly to Wendy. "And if Ms. Bedford wants a job that badly, I hope she gets one."

They parted. Wendy circulated for a few more minutes and left. She had an eight A.M. flight back to the Midwest, and she wanted an extra half-hour of sleep more than thirty additional minutes of Potomac hustle.

Sharon Bedford left the Polis hospitality suite somewhat later and went to her own room, next door to it. As she opened the door, she must have found on the floor just inside an envelope containing a fax that the front desk had sent up. The fax read:

> Now don't argue. You are NOT going to ride a bus all the way back to D.C. tomorrow. Checkout time isn't until noon. I'll be there at 11:45 to help you with your bags, and I'll drive you back in my Cadillac El Dorado with the nice soft leather seats and the CD console and the air conditioning. Plus, we'll stop for a decent meal along the way.
>
> Todd.

Bedford hung a card on the outside doorknob after making checkmarks indicating that a Continental breakfast should be delivered to her room between 9:15 and 9:30 the following morning. She left a wake-up call for 6:45.

Most of those who'd attended the conference were booked on one of two mid-morning flights back to D.C. The hotel's corridors were bustling from an early hour, and the police interviews permitted a thorough reconstruction of the busy Sunday morning outside Bedford's room.

Marciniak came by at 7:45. He knocked on Bedford's door, was admitted, and stayed inside for about twenty minutes. A lobbyist noticed his entrance, and a Senate Finance Committee staffer who was eager to check out in time to catch the 8:30 airport shuttle and was hustling down the hallway between 8:05 and 8:10 remembered Marciniak greeting him by name as Marciniak came out of Bedford's room.

At 8:15 Bedford called the kitchen and canceled her Continental breakfast order.

Jeffrey Quentin dropped by Bedford's room at 8:30 or slightly before. He was closeted with her for twenty minutes plus or minus a couple, making two calls from her room in response to messages on his beeper. By 9:05, Quentin was in the lobby with his attaché case and Samsonite soft-side suit carrier, checking out.

At 8:55 a maid noticed a card hanging on Bedford's doorknob, turned to expose the side reading MAID SERVICE PLEASE. The maid noted the request.

Bedford herself must have left her room around nine o'clock, because she'd already bought a *Washington Post* from the hotel's gift and magazine shop when she appeared in the Almost Heaven Cafe just before 9:10. At the café she ordered scrambled eggs, link sausage, white toast with grape jam, hash brown potatoes, black coffee, and a large glass of orange juice. Unlike the other, rather Spartan meals she'd eaten at the hotel since her arrival Friday evening, she paid for this rich and pricey repast with a hotel voucher. No one on the hotel staff could have said why Bedford was entitled to a voucher, but it didn't occur to anyone to ask.

She lingered with the *Post* over what, for her, was close to a banquet. When she finally presented the voucher, the café's cash register time-stamped it 10:02 A.M.

Around 10:15 or 10:20, a bellhop hustling a cartful of bags down the corridor noticed Scott Pilkington knock at Bedford's door. He didn't go in immediately, according to the bellhop. Instead, Bedford came out into the hallway, folded her arms across her chest, and conducted a brief and apparently rather frosty conversation with him. Only then did they both step inside and close the door. Within a couple of minutes Pilkington came out again and left.

There matters stayed until 11:40 A.M., when Todd Gallagher showed up.

Gallagher was conspicuous. He was six feet, three inches tall and weighed well over two hundred pounds. His forty-nine years had added only a speck or two of gray to dark brown hair that he wore short but combable. He had the quick, easy smile and bluff manner that makes savvy Southerners count their fingers after a handshake. His loden green cashmere sport coat fit over his muscular shoulders and broad chest with a perfection that bespoke custom tailoring. His khaki chinos might have come off the rack at JCPenney's. Noticing this, the experienced bellhop concluded correctly that Gallagher had lots of money and no wife.

Standing at the house phone in the lobby, Gallagher frowned through twenty rings on what the operator assured him was the phone in Bedford's room. After an unproductive tour of the lobby, bar, and the Almost Heaven Cafe, he tried again ten minutes later with the same result.

"She checked out yet?" he asked when the operator cut back in the second time.

"No, sir," the operator said crisply.

There are fifty ways to get a room number from a desk clerk and Gallagher used them all, passing a single bill with a portrait of President Grant on it. Taking the stairs to the second floor two at a time, he wasn't breathing hard when he swung to a stop outside Bedford's room.

If Bedford wasn't answering her phone, the odds were she wouldn't be responding to knocks on her door, either. Though he would have been wrong in this particular case, however, Gallagher might have been excused for believing that the average hotel room lock wouldn't be much of a challenge for the chief executive officer of SafeHome Security's most successful South Atlantic region franchisee. Which Gallagher happened to be.

He was destined, however, never to find out. After raising his right hand for a first, perfunctory rap, he froze with his knuckles an inch from the door. He realized that there was water leaking onto his tooled snakeskin boots from underneath the door.

chapter

5

★

Sharon Bedford lay in the bathtub, naked, in water that had filled the tub and overflowed it long enough for an oozing puddle to seep way all the way to the hallway door. A thick white towel sat bunched against the wall on the back of the tub, where she could have rested her head had she still been alive. In death—or perhaps shortly before—she had slipped along the tub's bottom, submerging her head and shoulders. More than an hour's worth of hot, running water had fogged the bathroom's several mirrors and accounted for the steamy, humid odor pervading the room.

To get into the room, once Gallagher had alerted him, the hotel security officer had used a universal key-card on the hallway door's principal lock. Then he'd had to jimmy the night-bolt with a pry bar and cut through the chain lock with bolt cutters. Neither the night-bolt nor the chain lock could be fastened from outside the room.

As soon as he'd turned off the water and confirmed that Bedford was dead, the security officer had called the police. While he did that, Gallagher had paced in agitated distraction around the small part of the room between the foot of the bed and the opposite wall. His eyes dull with shock, his pale lips moving in unheard mutterings, grief splashed with vivid eloquence across his features, he opened and closed massive fists and periodically snapped his head in a spasmodic shake.

During the intervals when he could concentrate at all, he sought refuge from his pain by meticulously cataloging what he saw in the small room. Pausing occasionally, he examined the adjoining door leading to the hospitality suite. The tongue-and-groove sliding latch on Bedford's side was shut. Gallagher, who knew something about the subject, couldn't see any sign that the latch or any part of the door frame had been forced. He saw instantly that the latch couldn't be closed from outside the room.

The windows were all shut and latched from the inside. Even if they hadn't been, it was clear that none of them could be opened wide enough for a human being to get in.

Bedford's suitcase lay open on the bed and looked about two-thirds packed. White cotton underpants and brassiere lay on the pillows. Two outfits were spread out on the bed, one on each side of the suitcase, as if Bedford had planned to decide after bathing which one to put on and which one to pack. Both were simple: white linen slacks and a round-necked cotton pullover on one side, a denim skirt and a short-sleeved blue blouse on the other. A pair of Adidas court shoes lay on the floor beside the bed.

A large purse of pearl gray vinyl sat on top of the low dresser that extended from the television cabinet. Beside it, trailing a power cord that dropped toward an outlet near the floor, a laptop computer nestled inside an open, black zipper case.

"This is a smoking room," Gallagher muttered, a suggestion of bafflement coloring the comment. "She didn't smoke."

The security officer, who'd been eyeing Gallagher warily since completing his phone call, nodded understandingly at the remark. His name was Harvey Barnstable. Out in the hallway, while Gallagher was explaining with considerable agitation why he should break the door down, Barnstable had learned that Gallagher had come to the hotel expecting to pick Bedford up, and that Bedford was very close to him. From a guy like Gallagher in a situation like this you expected shock or rage. Barnstable was relieved that it was going to be shock. He took two quick strides to where Gallagher was standing, trying to show his sympathy by physical closeness without actually touching Gallagher or doing anything else that might make him uncomfortable.

"Wife?" he asked.

"She was gonna be," Gallagher said. "She didn't know it yet, but she was gonna be."

"Were you coming up to ask her? God, that's tough."

"No, she had to get some things out of her system. I'd asked her twice and she'd said yes twice and then got cold feet twice. I figured on making the third one stick."

"Maybe we better step outside till the police get here?" Barnstable said, inflecting his voice at the end to make the sentence a strongly suggestive question.

"Huh? Oh, sure. Right."

The police hadn't arrived yet when Michaelson lugged his copies of the Sunday *New York Times* and *Washington Post* through the lobby at 12:10, but he knew something was wrong. His job for more than three decades had included picking up subtle cues in edgy body language and nervously elaborate speech that signaled some tense departure from routine. The tension might arise from something as oblique as an interior minister going into the hospital, or as dramatic as a bloody riot being planned. Whichever, when you were four thousand miles from home and the marines at the embassy were outnumbered a thousand to one by street thugs, it was a good idea to stay ahead of the curve.

The hair-trigger nervousness in the lobby seemed palpable to him. A senior assistant manager was staffing one of the slots at the registration desk, scanning the lobby with preoccupied glances as she dealt mechanically with the paperwork that came her way. The concierge offered an automatic smile to anyone venturing within two yards of his Louis Quinze table, but his ear stayed pinned to a telephone receiver, and when he spoke into it he resorted to whispered monosyllables. The bell captain stood his post, but he repeatedly adjusted the silver braid on his maroon cuffs and he looked like someone who very much wanted to find a bathroom.

Seating himself in a well-stuffed armchair that faced the registration desk, Michaelson pulled the Week in Review section from the *Times*. He read it with one eye while he watched the desk and the front door with the other.

From the corner of the reading eye he picked up a splash of royal blue. He looked up from the paper to see Scott Pilkington approach, wearing the casual shirt Michaelson had just glimpsed and a pair of brown slacks. The leisure wear was elegant enough, certainly, but without his worsted pinstripes Pilkington seemed for a moment jarringly out of his element, like MacArthur in mufti or Joe DiMaggio in hunting pinks.

"Checked out and waiting for a cab to the airport, I hope?" Pilkington asked quietly as without invitation he seated himself opposite Michaelson.

"No. I'm staying over another night, as a matter of fact."
Pilkington didn't try to hide his surprise at this revelation.

"West Virginia must have charms I hadn't fully appreciated."

"Two that come to mind are distance from Washington and distance from Washingtonians."

"Just a thought, but you may want to reconsider," Pilkington said.

"Why?"

"A couple of minutes ago I couldn't help noticing a rent-a-cop breaking into a room next door to last night's hospitality suite. He wasn't being shy about it, and from the urgency he brought to the operation, I surmised that he feared something pretty serious on the other side. I'm betting police, tedious questions, long delays, and other things that might very quickly take the bloom off West Virginia's placid rose. Almost everyone who came for the conference is gone, and any participant who's still around risks being seized on with avidity by cops who want information fast."

Folding the unfinished newspaper section resignedly on top of the pile on his lap, Michaelson gazed for several seconds at Pilkington.

"There must be more," he said at last. "What is it?"

"This is strictly a professional courtesy," Pilkington said briskly. "Favor for an alumnus, old times' sake, no strings attached, no ulterior motive. That sort of thing."

"Who was registered to the room in question?"

"A young woman named Bedburg or Bedford or something had it Friday and Saturday night. She may well have checked out by now. By great good luck she wasn't actually part of the conference, though I gather that she crashed several of the events."

Bedford. Michaelson closed his eyes and allowed himself a brief sigh.

"Thank you for the advice," he said then.

"Which you intend to ignore, I take it?"

"Which I intend to disregard. I don't think a sudden and conspicuous change of plans on my part is likely to reduce the interest of the local authorities in me. Quite the contrary. I have it on good authority that the guilty flee where no man pursueth."

Michaelson glanced over Pilkington's right shoulder and nodded briefly. Pilkington cranked his head around to look in the same direction. He saw a dark-haired woman who looked to be in her mid-forties and was in fact in her early fifties stroll with patrician serenity through the lobby and stop at the registration desk. A bellhop straining under the burden of two suitcases, an overnight case, and a canvas carryall staggered behind her. His face was a shade darker than the maroon trim on his uniform.

"Oh," Pilkington said. "I see."

"That verges on indiscretion," Michaelson said.

"What in the world does she have in the larger suitcase? An Olympic-class weight set?"

"Marjorie always takes her rock collection along for good luck."

"Still—all that for an overnight stay in Charleston?"

"You have just officially gone beyond verging. Actually, Marjorie is on her way back to Washington from the better part of a week at a booksellers' convention in Las Vegas. By the way, I want you to feel perfectly free to run along if you're anxious to avoid tedious questions and constabulary entanglements. If you can get through the next fifteen minutes without another subtly suggestive comment, I might even drop by after I get back to D.C. and give you a rundown on any informational tidbits that fall into my lap."

Two uniformed police officers and two men in civilian clothes hustled through the front door. One of the uniformed officers peeled off toward the registration counter. The rest of the group, directed with frantically discreet little waves by the concierge, hurried toward the stairs.

"Yes," Pilkington said. "I think I will be pushing off at that."

chapter

6

★

I'm betting you're intrigued in spite of yourself by that young woman's death," Marjorie said as she strolled with Michaelson along the Kanawha River toward the Radisson on the back leg of a relaxed evening walk.

"Almost the opposite of intrigued," Michaelson answered. "Except for your stimulating presence, I'd be feeling the way Gatsby did after Miss Buchanan left."

"Lackadaisical?"

"You know me too well."

With powerful *bongs* a carillon somewhere was punctuating the arrival of five in the evening. Marjorie and Michaelson had had several hours to learn in more detail than Pilkington had offered exactly what had brought the police hustling past Marjorie as she registered, for secrets are hard to keep in a hotel. They knew by now that Sharon Bedford had died in her room under circumstances that were at least puzzling and possibly suspicious.

"Would your enervation have something to do with the little chat you and Scott Pilkington were having when I arrived?"

"Yes. He was giving me advice."

"Which must have been tedious."

"And the advice was correct."

"Which must have been aggravating."

"Right on both counts," Michaelson said. Without further prompting, he told her what the advice was.

"Why do you think Pilkington's approach is the right one?" Marjorie asked.

"Charleston is a state capital that I'm sure has a perfectly competent police force. If Sharon Bedford's death involved anything more sinister than a pathetic suicide or an imprudent combination of drugs and alcohol, the best chance of finding that out is to let the local authorities investigate it as they would any other suspicious demise. Should reporters start tying her death to the conference or someone associated with it—even someone as little known as I am—then it certainly won't do that unfortunate person any good at all. More important, the murder turns into show business overnight, and any hopes of a serious investigation drastically diminish."

"You're right," Marjorie said deliberately, as if she was reluctant to accept the conclusion. "Or, rather, Pilkington's right. If Sharon Bedford's death becomes a national political issue instead of a local law-enforcement question, the detectives will spend more time answering questions from tabloid reporters than they will interviewing witnesses. It'd make the Vince Foster fiasco look like a model of professional police work."

Rounding a gentle curve, they spotted the gilded dome of West Virginia's capitol. They were less than a block from the hotel.

"I should probably be past worrying about the effect of political fallout on my own prospects but I'm not," Michaelson said. "Even if I were, there's Wendy to think about."

They walked in silence for the last hundred feet or so. The afternoon and the evening thus far had precisely met the modest expectations they'd had when they'd planned their meeting here. Lazy hours passed working acrostics and crosswords, eating a room-service meal, strolling through a pleasant slice of an America that was about as real to most people in Washington as Mark Twain's Missouri—this was exactly what they'd been hoping for.

Three years, Marjorie thought. No, more like four. Almost four years had passed since the last time Michaelson had talked to Marjorie about losing his wife. When he'd brought it up before, it had almost always been in settings like this, and she wondered if he was about to allude to it again.

She supposed she was the only one he ever talked to about "losing" Charlotte Michaelson. Most people would have taken him to mean that his wife had died. He didn't mean that, she knew. He meant that he'd lost her the way you lose a train of thought or lose track of what you're doing, through lapse of concentration and inattention. She didn't agree with him and had told him so, but she'd given up arguing about it with him.

An aphorism describes the ideal foreign service officer as "faithful, skillful, and exact, but above all not excessively zealous." Marjorie figured that Talleyrand had gotten it right when he'd turned that phrase a couple of centuries back. Excessive zeal got in the way of being skillful and exact. The first job of any foreign service officer is to get the facts right and analyze them with perfect dispassion, untinctured by comforting illusions or emotional revulsion or what the big guy down the street wanted to hear. The Pakistanis might be fine chaps whom President Nixon admired and the Indians might be insufferable hypocrites whom he despised, but that didn't mean Pakistan could stand up to India when the tanks rolled. Those are the facts, Mr. President. That's what the numbers on the ground say. Sorry you're disappointed, but making you feel good isn't in my job description.

Back then in the early seventies, the careerists said that Michaelson (along with several colleagues) had made the mistake of being right too early, leaving his career maimed if not destroyed. Cynics—in whose number Marjorie emphatically counted herself at the time—opined that that was why Charlotte Michaelson had left, figuring she'd never be an ambassador's wife.

Marjorie realized now that she'd been wrong. Charlotte had left because she couldn't face the thought of careening into her forties with a man who was faithful, skillful, and exact, but not excessively zealous. Who'd look at her without illusion or self-deception, who'd see her as she saw herself at two in the morning: a matron whose charm had turned brittle with the approach of middle age, whose once-lancing curiosity had atrophied in the dreary days after Washington went from Camelot to California east, who now treated *The New York Times Book Review* as Cliff Notes for cocktail party conversation. She'd left Richard not because of his weakness but because of his greatest strength and her icy fear that she was unequal to it.

And Michaelson had blamed himself, Marjorie knew. He'd felt that he should have sensed the unspoken anguish, should have found a way to restore his wife's disintegrating spirit, to show her that he loved her as a woman and not a credential or an ornament. Nixon he could forgive; himself, for many years, he couldn't.

Marjorie understood what searing pain the divorce had produced, and if she'd been granted some fairy-tale power to spare Michaelson that yawning ache, she would have. At the same time, though, she wondered what he'd be like now if he hadn't gone through it, if he hadn't experienced that single transcendent failure and that long black night of self-doubt. Would he have turned into a slightly less obnoxious version of Pilkington, with intelligence a mile wide and an inch deep, clever but not wise, bright but not thoughtful, recycling prefabricated quips, trading on carefully rehearsed spontaneity, confusing power with strength, knowledge with judgment, verbal facility with vision?

She didn't know. She did know that the end result of Michaelson's trauma was someone whose instincts she trusted. She would have trusted him in a situation room, making decisions while lieutenant colonels moved model ships around a map board. And she trusted him in a hotel lobby, letting her know he was there but not jumping on her the moment she walked in and signaling to every bellhop in the vicinity that she'd come to a tryst.

Michaelson held the door open for Marjorie as they reached the Radisson, and was still a step or two behind her when they began to cross the lobby. He was startled when a man even taller than he and far huskier suddenly loomed in front of him.

"Excuse me, sir," the man said in something just north of a drawl, with a very slight slurring on the two *s*'s. "I would appreciate a word with you, please."

Michaelson checked his first instinct, which was to say,

"Certainly. How about sometime when you're sober?" The abruptness of the man's approach and the almost exaggerated politeness of his diction couldn't hide the keening anguish wrapped around his words, his tone, the expression on his face. He might be drunk or close to it, but he deserved better than dinner party repartee.

"This is Marjorie Randolph," Michaelson said, gesturing toward his companion, who had turned back and was looking questioningly at the scene. "I'm Richard Michaelson, as you presumably know. I'm afraid I can't carry the introductions any further than that."

"My apologies, ma'am," the man said to Marjorie with apparently deep sincerity. "I didn't realize you were with this gentleman, or I wouldn't have intruded this way."

"That's quite all right," Marjorie said. Michaelson noticed with some amusement that Marjorie's own tidewater accent slipped a couple of degrees toward Tara. "And I have the pleasure of being introduced to whom, please?"

"Todd Gallagher, ma'am." The man bowed slightly.

Michaelson considered offering to go for mint juleps.

"If you'll excuse me for interrupting," he said instead, "the word you'd like to have with me concerns Sharon Bedford, correct?"

"Yessir," Gallagher confirmed, wheeling back to face Michaelson. "Once the cops got through with me, I greased the hired help enough to find out that you're about the only one here for the conference that hadn't hightailed it out of town."

"Relative?" Michaelson asked. "Friend? Associate?"

"Friend," Gallagher said. The syllable was almost a moan, Gallagher's voice throbbing with pain as he spoke it.

"I'm very sorry for your loss," Michaelson said. "I don't

know that I can offer much consolation. I only met Ms. Bedford in passing. But if you think it would help to talk to someone who was here this weekend, I'm happy to do it. If you're staying over, perhaps tomorrow morning would be a good time."

"Excuse me for interrupting," Marjorie said, "but it occurs to me that if I weren't here, you two would be having your talk immediately, and I think that that's what ought to happen."

"No, no," Gallagher said almost shyly. "I know three's a crowd. I just—"

"Not a bit of it," Marjorie said, her voice a model of brook-no-nonsense feminine firmness. "I've had Richard's undivided attention for the last four hours, and I can certainly share him for the next ninety minutes or so." She glanced at her watch. "Just give me a chance to comb my hair. Richard, I'll knock on your door in seven minutes."

With that she strode toward the elevators, exuding a regal confidence so complete that footmen trailing in her wake would have seemed superfluous.

His head spinning a bit from the delicate finesse that had turned his intended confrontation of Michaelson into a three-party conversation without his ever quite realizing what was happening, Gallagher stood with Michaelson for over a minute, waiting to no purpose he could discern. He couldn't have been expected to know that by "combing my hair" Marjorie had meant closing the connecting doors between the adjoining rooms that she and Michaelson had. The weighty suitcase that had caught Pilkington's attention when Marjorie checked in lay open on the bed in Marjorie's room, its load of thirty-two brand-new hardcover books displayed for random perusal. The clear implication was that Marjorie wouldn't be using that bed herself. She didn't really think that this would scandalize Gallagher, but she saw no reason to take any chances.

"Why did she break the first two off?" Marjorie asked Gallagher once they were well into the conference in Michaelson's room that they'd arranged improvisationally in the lobby. Michaelson realized that this was a question he wouldn't have considered asking. He was surprised and intrigued when it pulled a smile from Gallagher.

"She thought I was too good for her," he said. "Swear to God. Buried one wife, six kids going from a Sunday-school teacher to a fighter pilot to a bouncer in a roadhouse, just a big old salesman who got lucky, and she acted like I was a combination of Joe Willie Namath and Robert E. Lee."

"Most women I know," Marjorie said carefully, "would have found a way to deal with that."

"Most women aren't Sharon." Gallagher took a long drink from a bottle of Budweiser. "She saw a picture of me from 'Nam in my ranger outfit and she couldn't get over it. Like I was a Green Beret or something. I told her I was nothing special, maybe half a step above an MP, but it was just exactly like talking to that wall over there. There wasn't any way I was gonna make myself into a normal human being in her eyes, so I had to hope she'd get herself up into the same kind of category she was putting me in."

"Which meant a job back on the inside," Michaelson said.

"Yessir. She never really got over losing her NSC job. She had decent enough jobs after that, but she couldn't stay interested in something where the most important thing you did was clear your desk by Friday afternoon."

"Where was she working most recently?" Marjorie asked.

"Self-employed. Summarizing depositions for shorthanded law firms, mostly. Some technical writing, putting stuff written by propeller heads in language ordinary people could understand."

Gallagher settled back on his perch at the windowsill and drank more beer. Two Buds after confronting Michaelson in the lobby, Gallagher seemed considerably more sober now than he had then. He also appeared calmer, meeting Bedford's death no longer with shock but with a deep, gradual, sorrowing acceptance.

"I'm afraid I haven't been able to provide much consolation," Michaelson said apologetically.

"That's okay." Rising, Gallagher dropped the now-empty bottle into a wastebasket and stretched his long arms and legs a bit. "Just talking about Sharon has helped a lot. I really appreciate your putting up with me."

"That's entirely all right," Michaelson said. "I do have one bit of information for you, and one piece of advice that you can take for whatever you think it's worth."

"Shoot."

"Ms. Bedford looked me up yesterday evening. She wanted my help in going after one of the jobs she was interested in. She had a very definite idea about what I could do for her, and she wanted to see me after I got back to Washington."

"Doesn't sound despondent to me," Gallagher said.

"I agree. When a physically healthy young woman dies alone in a locked room, you can't help thinking of suicide, but I'd require a great deal of convincing to accept that hypothesis in this case."

"Thank you," Gallagher said. "That helps. It truly does."

"You may find my advice less appealing," Michaelson said. "I suggest that you wait—that you give the police a few days to investigate Ms. Bedford's death before you jump in."

"Jump in how?"

"Hiring a private investigator. Tracking down a witness or two and bracing them. Peddling a conspiracy theory to the press."

Gallagher chuckled and eased his hips comfortably back against the wall. Raising his left hand, he idly stroked a fringe of overlong whisker-stubble at the back of his jaw.

"What in the world makes you think I have anything like that in mind?" he asked in the kind of voice people use to ask how fast they were going, Officer.

"Wild guess," Michaelson said, smiling.

"You'll have to do better than that if you expect me to pay attention."

"You've spent most of fifty years going hard after whatever really mattered to you. I think Sharon Bedford was the most important thing in your life for the last year or so, and to have her ripped away from you so brutally has to be devastating. You need to believe there's something you can *do* about that. You can do something about a murderer, but you can't do anything about an embolism that popped up in the wrong place or some other random absurdity. Right now there's only one explanation for her death that you're psychologically capable of accepting—and that's a bad frame of mind to be in when you're making tactical decisions."

"I want to show you something," Gallagher said, pulling out his wallet. "Sharon mailed it to my home address Thursday—the day she left for the conference here."

He handed Michaelson a roughly hand-sized piece of paper

that he extracted from the wallet. Marjorie leaned over as Michaelson held the paper in the light so that they could both read the blue ink notations on it:

101248
152237
KISSINGER
4939
HIGHWAYS TO INDIANS
2612

"Do you have any idea what this is?" Michaelson asked.

"It's a paper she generally kept posted on her refrigerator door with a little ladybug magnet," Gallagher said, his voice catching for a fraction of a second at the end. "I recognize most of the things on there. The top number happens to be the combination to her bicycle lock. Four-nine-three-nine was her PIN number for automatic teller machines. The bottom number is the code that turns off the security system I installed at her apartment."

"What about 'Kissinger'?" Marjorie asked.

"Security system again," Gallagher said. "It's a disregard code. If the alarm goes off, the office calls your place pronto. If you say, 'Everything's okay,' the office assumes there's a guy standing there with a knife at your throat and calls the cops. If everything really is okay and you'd just set the alarm off by mistake, you give your disregard code and the office forgets the whole thing. Sharon picked 'Kissinger' for hers."

"The second number looks like a padlock combination, too," Marjorie said.

"Could be," Gallagher agreed. "Might be a gym locker or her bin in the storage area of her building, or something else."

"Which leaves 'Highways to Indians,' " Michaelson said.

"Don't have a clue about that one," Gallagher said, shrugging.

"Provocative," Michaelson said.

"If that means it smells funny, I agree with you," Gallagher said. "Why would she have gone to the trouble to mail this thing off to me just before she came out to this conference?"

"An obvious possibility is that she didn't want it to be found if someone searched her apartment," Michaelson said.

"Searched it either while she was away or after something happened to her here," Gallagher added. "It looks to me like she thought that whatever she was peddling out here was risky. And it looks to me like maybe she was right."

"All the more reason to take my advice," Michaelson said.

"Why? What's going to change in a week?"

"In a week the police might be in hot pursuit of a murderer, if there was a murder. You can probably sell security systems better than they can, and they can probably investigate murders better than you."

"Uh-huh," Gallagher said. "And what if in a week they've just shrugged it off? Unexplained death of a nobody from out of town. Heart stopped beating. One a those things. Sharon Bedford becomes three pages stuck in a manila folder in some file cabinet."

"In that case," Michaelson said after a delicate pause, "if you still want to go after it, I'll help you." Crossing the room, he handed Gallagher his business card. "Give me a call. I know my way around Washington. I have a long memory, a fat Rolodex, and a lot of chits to call in."

Gallagher accepted the card and pressed one corner thoughtfully against the dimple in his chin.

"Why are you offering to do something like that?" he asked.

"I'm not really sure," Michaelson said with a brief shrug. "Maybe I had a few more beers than usual because of a woman once."

"The offer's good only if I take your advice, is that it?"

"Quid pro quo, as we used to say in the foreign service."

"All right," Gallagher said decisively, holding out his hand, "you got yourself a deal. Three hours ago I'd'a bet next month's paycheck there wasn't a better salesman than me in Charleston tonight, and son of a gun if I wouldn't have lost."

They shook hands. Gallagher touched Michaelson's card just above his right eyebrow by way of taking his leave of Marjorie, and left the room. Marjorie waited for five seconds after the door had closed behind him before she spoke.

"You've abused subordinates, the English language, yours truly, and a lot of other things over a woman," she piped then reproachfully, "but alcohol isn't one of them. That had to be the most transparent lie you've ever told."

"Actually," Michaelson said, "I believe I told a slightly more transparent lie to the Saudi oil minister in 1978. He didn't believe me, though, so perhaps it doesn't count."

"What are you looking for?" she asked as he began rummaging through an attaché case that sat open on the bed.

"Scott Pilkington's number at work. I want to leave a message on his voice mail so that he'll get it first thing tomorrow. Mention that a cowboy's about to ride through his little patch with a very large amount of money and a very small amount of discretion."

"Do you anticipate adding something to the effect that where this particular cowboy's concerned you have the last ticket to the ball, so if Pilkington wants to come he'll have to dance with you?"

"That might come up," Michaelson said. "*If* I can find that blessed number."

"Here," Marjorie said, offering him a palm-sized computer.

Michaelson took the machine and saw Pilkington's number blinking on the screen.

"You did see this coming, didn't you?" he commented as he picked up the phone.

"As soon as he pulled that piece of paper out."

Marjorie waited patiently while Michaelson completed the call and left his message.

"Now," she said when he'd finished. "Would you please tell me the real reason you're doing what you carefully explained to me earlier this evening was exactly the wrong thing to do?"

"I'm at an age for sunsets and poetry," Michaelson said. "I'm not going to save the world or renew the country's spirit or even demilitarize the oil routes. But maybe I can keep one man from going bitter and obsessed into the last half of his middle age."

"Fair enough," Marjorie said. "A bit romantic for a hardheaded, unsentimental realist in his sixties, but fair enough."

"I still remember the action stateside twenty-five years ago when the Bengali uprising broke out in what was then East Pakistan," Michaelson said. "When things finally got too dicey, we sent the standard evacuation order to our mission in Dacca: 'women, children, and nonessential men.'" He glanced over at Marjorie, meeting her eyes. "I may be in my sixties, but I'm not quite ready for the nonessential men category yet."

Pilkington didn't call until Wednesday. When he did, he wanted to know if, by any wild chance, the Gallagher chap mentioned in Michaelson's voice-mail message had followed up. Michaelson said that as a matter of fact he had.

"And?" Pilkington prompted.

"Barring a police breakthrough in the Bedford investigation, we're meeting on Sunday."

"Then you and I had better meet on Saturday."

"Where and when?" Michaelson asked.

"Fourish at Dunsinane."

"Don't you think Dunsinane is overdoing it a bit?"

"No doubt. See you there."

Michaelson hadn't been idle while he waited for Pilkington's call. He'd talked at length to Wendy Gardner, for example. What she told him would have meant little if Pilkington hadn't called. When Pilkington did call, though, Wendy's information told Michaelson that he should try to talk to Jerry Marciniak before his meeting with Pilkington.

Michaelson arranged to do this early Friday morning. Very early.

"Ninety percent of science is waiting," Marciniak said without looking up from the microscope when Michaelson appeared in the lab's doorway.

"So is ninety percent of getting to see you," Michaelson said. "That and getting out of bed before dawn."

"This baby's not ready to tell us anything yet," Marciniak said as he slipped a glass slide from the viewing tray and tucked it between two holders in a ceramic case a few feet away on the long, slate table. Slipping off the stool where he'd been perched, he strode briskly across the large room's echoing tile floor.

"Between seven-fifteen and eight-thirty is the only time I can actually do hands-on science here in the lab," he said. "From then on it's paperwork, committee meetings, and making nice with politicians. Let's go to my office."

Michaelson followed Marciniak through a swinging double door and down a long, institutional gray hallway. Marciniak's cardigan sweater this morning was red, his dress shirt blue and neatly pressed but open at the neck.

"What's your reaction to Sharon Bedford's death?" Michaelson asked.

"It's a shame she's dead, and the way she died stinks out loud. I've asked for a copy of the autopsy report."

They stepped into a sunlit office, rather spacious by GSA standards but seeming cramped because of the piles of paper, books, reports, and pale green-jacketed files that filled the desk, shelves, floor, windowsills, and two of the chairs.

"My office doesn't usually look this bad," Marciniak said

offhandedly as he circled behind his desk. "It usually looks worse. Sorry, old joke. See if you can find a place to sit."

Michaelson obeyed the instruction, transferring a top-heavy paper tower from a chair to the floor.

"What bothers you about the way Ms. Bedford died?" he asked.

"You've got a reasonably healthy young woman without any obvious bad habits who's eating breakfast and walking around like nothing's wrong one minute and the next thing anyone knows her heart stops beating. You don't have to be Quincy to figure we're not talking about natural causes here."

"Just a doctor's professional curiosity, then?" Michaelson prompted.

"A *scientist's* professional curiosity," Marciniak corrected him. "My M.D. proved I have a memory. It was my Ph.D. that proved I have a mind."

Michaelson nodded deferentially.

"You didn't know Sharon Bedford before the conference, though?" he asked.

"Matter of fact, I did know her," Marciniak said. "She'd talked to me about getting a serious policy-area job somewhere. She got to be a gluteal pain about it, in fact. I mean, she was hungry and I can understand that, but it gets old after a while. She thought we'd be doing her a favor to let her work fifty hours a week for thirty-two thousand a year, but I can't just snap my fingers and make something like that happen."

"Do you have any idea why she picked you as a possible job contact?"

"I had a pulse, for one thing," Marciniak said. "She'd network with anyone who was breathing regularly, and I qualified. Plus, I'd done in spades what she was trying to do in clubs. I elbowed my way from glorified desk clerk to a senior policy-making job. I guess she figured I'd empathize."

"Did you?"

"I suppose so. I see classmates in the private sector at outfits like Triangle Research, making twice my top government salary, flying first class, staying at hotels that you couldn't even see a Holiday Inn from, driving a Lexus provided by their companies—and you know what? I wouldn't trade places with them. I couldn't stand to be out of it, away from the action. So sure, I understood her feeling the same way."

"Do you know how she happened to get so knowledgeable about your career?" Michaelson asked. "The through-the-hawse-hole stuff, I mean."

"Now, I'm gonna sound like an egomaniac, but what the hell. They knew my name over there at NSC when she was there. There's a computer entry over there saying I'm a whiz about institutional dynamics in mature bureaucracies. Swear to God, and don't ask me why. They had me in for a chat when they were noodling over some big-picture metatheory called the Mandarin Hypothesis."

"I'm afraid I'm drawing a blank on that one," Michaelson said.

Leaning back so far in his chair that the front legs lifted off the carpet, Marciniak flicked his right hand carelessly.

"The premise is that every society starts out just barely getting by. Subsistence. Then, boom, something no one understands happens and suddenly some societies explode with energy, going farther in two generations than they had in six centuries. Whatever it is that happens has something to do with people who are really good at doing something useful: fighting, growing food, making tools, putting ten million bits

of information on a ceramic chip the size of your fingernail—
that kind of thing."

"I'm with you," Michaelson said, nodding.

"The hypothesis is that just when things are going really
well, something strange happens. Power starts slipping away
from people who can *do* things and passes to people who can
say things. Priests in Egypt and ancient Israel. Mandarins in
China. *Fonctionnaires* and bureaucrats in prerevolutionary
France. *Apparatchiks* in postrevolutionary Russia."

"Lawyers in the United States?" Michaelson asked a trifle
mischievously.

"You said it, I didn't. Anyway, that's the Mandarin Hypothesis. There really is a paper on it over there at NSC and I
suppose my name really does show up in a footnote somewhere. I think Sharon Bedford probably heard of me when
they were batting the thing around on a slow day in the White
House basement a few years back."

"It's quite stimulating," Michaelson said, "but I don't see
any obvious way to use it to explain why she died and who
killed her."

"No," Marciniak agreed, emphatically shaking his head.
"The Mandarin Hypothesis is a telescope. To get to the bot-
tom of whatever happened to her, you'll need a microscope.
Facts. Data."

"No doubt you're right," Michaelson said. "What did you
go to see her about the morning she died? That would qualify
as a datum, wouldn't it?"

"Fair enough." Marciniak shook his head with a half-smile.
"I had a lead on a job for her. Down the road, in an agency that
doesn't exist yet."

"An agency run by you?"

"It'd be nice if it worked out that way, but you learn not to count on things like that in this town."

"Sounds a tiny bit thin."

"Damn near invisible. I knew how bad she wanted it, though, so I thought I'd float it by her."

"How did she react?" Michaelson asked.

"She was more intrigued than I thought she'd be. She asked me for details, said she wanted to follow up."

"Not exactly the depths of despair, then."

"I never saw her despondent," Marciniak said. "Certainly not that weekend."

"Did she mention any inducement she could offer?" Michaelson asked. "Information that might come in handy for a busy senior official, that kind of thing?"

"Not to me she didn't. That'd be a pretty low-rent play. And anyway, I don't see how she could have had anything I wanted."

Michaelson saw the message-waiting light on Marciniak's phone begin to glow bright red. The bureaucratic day was about to start. He rose from his chair.

"If she had had something you wanted," he asked as he leaned across the desk to shake Marciniak's hand, "do you think you might have found a job that already existed for her?"

"Hey," Marciniak answered, grinning, "I said it was a low-rent play. I didn't say I was too classy to try it if it looked like it might work."

Not on Wimbledon's center court, not surrounding the sixteenth hole at Augusta, nowhere had Michaelson ever seen a lawn with the utterly level, glasslike smoothness and emerald

perfection of the bowling green at Dunsinane Driving and
Hunt Club in Chevy Chase. Four men in dazzling white flan-
nels stood or bent or crouched at one end of the square of turf,
contemplating with solemn gravity four solid black balls that
looked to be about sixteen inches around, and one smaller
white ball.

With something less than solemn gravity, Michaelson
watched them from the south patio immediately behind the
larger wing of the clubhouse. He took a deliberate and substantial sip from a heavy tumbler that had started off with two
fingers of undiluted Johnny Walker Black Label scotch.

"I take it that at some point one of them is actually going
to do something," he said to Pilkington, who sat with his own
glass of scotch on the other side of a white metal table.

"Don't be so provincial," Pilkington said. "If this were
baseball, there'd be just as much standing around and you'd
be lecturing me about how it's all part of the mental game."

"If this were baseball, the sphere would be moving a hundred and thirty-five feet per second. Doing something with it
would be intrinsically more impressive."

"It's a good thing you disregarded my advice about Sharon
Bedford," Pilkington said abruptly.

"I took your advice, actually. I volunteered nothing, and if
my profile had been any lower, I'd have been horizontal. But
Gallagher still tracked me down and insisted on conversation.
I enlisted only to avoid the draft."

"However your involvement came about, it's a stroke of
very good luck. I've spent a good part of the past week in
contact with the Charleston Police Department. It's gratifying
how ready they are to help the State Department. We apparently aren't quite as pushy as the FBI. At any rate, this thing

is shaping up as a four-alarm shambles for several people, including some whose good opinion I covet."

"Rather inconvenient for Ms. Bedford, too."

"She's past caring about it," Pilkington said. "The people I referred to are not."

"I'm all ears," Michaelson said.

"Poison. Bufotenine. Ingested orally."

"In English, please. You mean she swallowed a pill or took the poison in food or something?"

"Candy, in all probability. It looks like the last thing she ate was a chocolate mint that the maid left on her pillow after she cleaned the room up, and the betting is that that's what carried the poison. She was diabetic and nibbled frequently on sweets, as many diabetics do. She presumably ate the mint in one bite, climbed into the filling tub, and died."

"It doesn't sound much like accidental death," Michaelson said.

"I can't argue with that. Unfortunately, the answer that makes the most sense to me is a bit complicated."

"Suicide?"

"Yes."

Michaelson gazed at the lawn-bowlers for a long moment over a contemplative sip of scotch as he considered the possibility.

"It strikes me as a lot of trouble to take just to push off, and a pretty unpleasant way to do it," he said. "Besides that, I talked to the woman Saturday evening. She simply wasn't in that frame of mind."

"If you want to make her death murder, you have two choices," Pilkington said patiently. "One is to figure out a motive for the maid who cleaned the room while Ms. Bedford was at breakfast Sunday morning. She left a pillow mint in every room she cleaned, and there's no doubt the one Bedford swallowed was like the mints the hotel buys for that purpose. There was no mint when the police searched the room, and there was one and only one empty mint wrapper in the wastebasket."

"What's two?"

"Two is to come up with a way someone could have gotten into Bedford's room, between the time the maid left and the time Bedford came back from breakfast, without being noticed by anyone else and without Ms. Bedford realizing he'd been there."

"Pass-card?" Michaelson suggested.

"The maids and the front desk personnel had them, of course. But except for the one who cleaned, they all deny going into her room that morning, or providing a pass-card to anyone else on any pretext. When Gallagher and the hotel security officer found Bedford's body, the hallway door and the door communicating with the adjoining room were both locked from the inside. The windows were all closed, and anyway the maximum opening on any of them was only four inches. Far too small for a human being to get in or out."

"Marjorie mentioned that Philo Vance confronted a problem like this in *The Canary Murder Case*," Michaelson said. "According to her exposition, the murderer in that story used a slipknot in a length of thread to throw an inside bolt from outside the door."

"I've never heard of anyone having that kind of luck with a slipknot in real life," Pilkington said, "but let that go. The hallway door here was secured by three locks before Bedford indulged her sweet tooth for the last time: a standard lock, a night-bolt tripped by a lever just below the inside doorknob, and a chain lock about eye level on the door. The standard lock would be engaged simply by closing the door, but the other two could be locked only from the inside, and I don't see how you could do the thread trick on either of them."

"Neither do I," Michaelson said. "Marjorie and I spent a good hour Monday morning playing with the identical locks on my hotel room door. There's not the slightest doubt in my mind that Ms. Bedford secured those inside locks herself."

"So," Pilkington said. "That leaves someone getting in, somehow or other, during Bedford's breakfast."

"Only the standard lock would be engaged while she was in the café, presumably," Michaelson said. "Gallagher was sure he could have picked it. Perhaps that's what the murderer did."

"The police found no sign of that. More important, the corridor outside Bedford's room was like a Beltway rush hour Sunday morning. People who'd come to the conference were bustling around, trying to get to the airport for one of the morning flights back to Washington. Goings and comings around Bedford's room were noted. Extensively. Picking even a simple lock is a fairly conspicuous activity. It's hard to believe that that wouldn't have been spotted along with everything else, if it had happened."

"Is that the case for suicide, then?" Michaelson asked. "That she must've killed herself because we can't figure out how anyone else would have killed her?"

"I think it was a suicide with a purpose," Pilkington said. "I think she killed herself because she realized in the cold gray light of dawn that her thoughts of getting a significant government job back were pipe dreams. And I think she decided that as long as she was going to go, she might as well make trouble for the kind of people she blamed for her own bitter disappointments."

"You, for example?" Michaelson asked.

"No, as a matter of fact. I think her target was Jeffrey Quentin."

"What makes you say that?"

Pilkington drew a quarter-folded page from his shirt pocket and handed it to Michaelson. Unfolding the paper, Michaelson saw the cover and inside page of a birthday card photocopied on a single sheet. The card's cover showed a charming female tot, gamboling amidst flowers and balloons. Spaced over the inside page, in the kind of perfect script that used to be seen above the blackboards in elementary school rooms, was a single sentence.

" 'Your Little Girl Is One Year Old Today and She's Praying for You in Heaven,' " Michaelson read aloud. "*Disputandum de gustibus non* and all that, but it seems a bit grotesque."

"It was sent to women in the Wilmot, Ohio, area several years ago, approximately a year after they'd had abortions."

"In that case, not only grotesque but theologically unsound, at least if Augustine had things straight."

"The cards were sent to twelve women from late September through the third week in October," Pilkington explained. "In a year divisible by two."

"I see," Michaelson said.

"Two of the recipients suffered nervous breakdowns. One attempted suicide. Local media picked the story up and ran with it big time. Huge controversy erupted. The differences between the area's congressional candidates on abortion were microscopic, but this story injected abortion into the race and magnified those differences dramatically. They had a record turnout for an off-year election."

"Punchline?" Michaelson demanded with a trace of impatience.

"The campaign of the winning candidate was managed by Jeffrey Quentin."

"You, of course, are not implying, but I will infer, that Quentin was responsible for engineering this mailing, presumably through some cover group."

"If you could prove that," Pilkington said, "I think Mr. Quentin would have to find office space farther away from the White House than his current quarters."

"What does this have to do with Sharon Bedford?"

"One of the cards was found in her room. This is a photocopy of it."

"Was she one of the women victimized by this atrocity?"

"We can be quite certain she was not," Pilkington said. "The autopsy showed that Sharon Bedford had never been pregnant."

"Perhaps a sister, a close relative, or an old friend, then," Michaelson speculated.

"No reason to think so. Neither her life nor her circle of acquaintances seems to have intersected that part of the country. I think the explanation lies elsewhere."

"Namely?"

"She got her hands on that card and knew its history," Pilkington said. "She made the same inference you did. Then she tried to pry a job out of Quentin by claiming that she could conclusively tie him to it."

"And got nowhere."

"And got nowhere. He probably laughed in her face. He

undoubtedly treated her with complete contempt. When she realized that her rather pathetic ploy wasn't going to work, she decided in despair to jump off a cliff—and to grab his collar on the way down."

"What do you mean by grabbing his collar?" Michaelson asked. "The card by itself proves nothing about Quentin."

"Quentin, the card, and a tragedy all show up in Wilmot, Ohio," Pilkington explained. "Quentin, the card, and a tragedy all show up a few years later in West Virginia. Maybe it stimulates some journalistic curiosity somewhere and makes things inconvenient for Mr. Quentin. It's not much, but maybe it was all she had."

"Your theory is suspiciously convenient for those who'd like a nonculpable explanation for Ms. Bedford's death," Michaelson said.

"I can't help that. The facts are what they are."

"And one of the things they are is provocatively implausible in key respects."

"Example?" Pilkington demanded.

"No note."

"It happens."

"You're right," Michaelson said. "Something subconscious is making me look for excuses to resist your theory."

"Well, I hope you can overcome it. I suspect that Mr. Gallagher's resistance will be formidable enough by itself."

"It will. His work brings him to the Washington area one week a month as it is, and I think he's planning on dropping by even more frequently until Ms. Bedford's death is cleared up to his satisfaction."

"I have a role in mind for you in dealing with the Gallagher problem, actually," Pilkington said.

"What do you want me to do? And why do you expect me to do it?"

"I want you to help Gallagher accept the truth—no matter how unpalatable he may find it. I expect you to do it because it's the right thing to do from the standpoint of everyone involved."

"The truth? Or your theory about the truth?"

"Let the chips fall where they may," Pilkington said, waving his left hand expansively and then dropping it back to the table. "If you uncover something that shows I'm wrong, I'd like to be the first to hear about it, but I certainly don't want you to suppress it. That should go without saying."

"I'm nevertheless glad to hear you say it."

"You'll do it, then?"

"I'm going to do my best to help Gallagher understand what happened to a woman he loved very much. To do it right, I'll need your help. For one thing, I'll need information—access to yours, and your help in getting access to others'."

"Can do," Pilkington said.

"Second, I'll need cover."

"For whom?"

"Deborah Moodie, to begin with."

"That's harder."

"If it were easy," Michaelson said, "I could get it from Jeffrey Quentin."

"I'll see what I can do."

"In exchange for what I need, I'll give you the cooperation you're asking for. So. Once you're confident that you can deliver, give me a call. I take it you have my number?"

"The tape of your voice-mail message has been preserved," Pilkington said dryly.

What this guy Pilkington told you about Quentin bothers me a lot," Gallagher said, taking his eyes briefly off the road to glance at Michaelson.

"It bothers me as well," Michaelson said.

He pushed himself deeper into the corner of the El Dorado's rear right seat in an effort to avoid the arctic breeze from its array of air-conditioning vents. He had just finished summarizing his talk the day before with Pilkington.

"It sounds to me like Quentin had a pretty good reason to kill Sharon," Gallagher said.

"I'm not ready to buy the Quentin blackmail theory yet," Michaelson said.

"Why not?"

"For one thing," Marjorie said from the front passenger seat, "the idea that exposing Quentin's role in that abortion atrocity would ruin him strikes some informed people as unmitigated nonsense."

"Thus spake Wendy?" Michaelson asked.

"Approximately. She used a colorful synonym for nonsense."

"Who's Wendy?" Gallagher asked.

"Wendy Gardner," Michaelson said. "A friend."

"A friend who's actually won an election or two," Marjorie added, "and who's been indirectly involved in electoral politics since she was about six."

"Did she explain or are you just taking her word for it?" Gallagher demanded.

"Wendy pointed out that, however reprehensible morally, the abortion ploy was tactically brilliant. After all, as she observed, it worked. Assuming that Sharon could plausibly have threatened to tag Jeffrey Quentin with it, that wouldn't have hurt him in his chosen profession, it would have helped him. It probably wouldn't have gotten him bounced from the White House staff, and even if it did, he'd still be more in demand as a campaign consultant than ever."

"That's kind of depressing," Gallagher said.

"Not the first time the truth has been depressing," Michaelson said. "Besides, the card Ms. Bedford had come across was left in the room. If Quentin had killed her to cover up that part of his past, he'd presumably at least have taken the thing with him."

"I don't know," Gallagher said. "Maybe she had something else in the room a lot more conclusive than the card, and maybe he did take that. Besides, he was there and he's a slimebag. I can't see clearing him."

"I'm not clearing him," Michaelson said. "I'm just saying there's no evidence so far that he's the murderer. We don't have any real basis yet for focusing on anyone as a suspect."

Gallagher's body language suggested no acquiescence in this assessment, but he didn't continue to challenge it. Instead he pulled the Cadillac to a smooth stop across the street from a collection of what an elegant sign called town houses, crowded onto two almost treeless acres. The sign explained that each town house contained four "Completely Private Living Units."

"Here we are," he said. "This is where Sharon lived. Number two-fourteen."

The police hadn't sealed 214, and apparently no one had changed the locks, because keys Gallagher had got them in and turned off the alarm. They stepped directly into a musty living room. The room was orderly, but there was a hasty, improvised quality to its neatness, as if it were the result of half an hour's scurrying just before Bedford left for the bus station.

A computer desk with a Compudyne computer, monitor, keyboard, and printer dominated the far wall. A small radio in a turquoise Bakelite housing rested on the desk's far corner. Marjorie crossed over and flipped it on. "Yesterday" came out in instrumental cover, arranged for elevator with strings heavy and sweet.

A handful of framed pictures and certificates hanging above the desk drew Michaelson's attention. Fifteen years before, Sharon Bedford had graduated with honors from Stuyvesant Public High School in Deming, New York. Five years after that SUNY at Stonybrook had given her a bachelor's degree in political science. In one color picture Bedford in cap and gown stood between a Jell-O-cheeked man with steel-framed glasses and a wiry, bland-faced woman who wore her dark hair like Jackie Kennedy's.

Two four-shelf, screw-together metal bookshelves stood against the wall to the right. Michaelson spotted computer manuals and a collection of White House memoirs—the bulky kind that he had assumed were bought mostly to be given away rather than read: Reagan's, McFarlane's, Kissinger's (both volumes), and Quayle's, with Peggy Noonan thrown in. Bedford was also a big Tom Clancy fan, mixing copies of his books in with the memoirs. And she'd had what looked like a complete set of Erle Stanley Gardner's Perry Mason stories in paperback. Beyond that, her tastes seemed to run to the kind of fiction that Michaelson had heard Marjorie classify as Contemporary Sentimental Education: Jackie Collins, Danielle Steel, and several names boasting similar arrays of sibilants and labiants.

Michaelson had expected to feel pity and he'd armed himself against it. Pity was useless. Welling up in him now, though, was a different and more dangerous emotion. He felt an angry frustration, not at her death so much as at what seemed the almost capricious casualness of that death.

Sharon Bedford had been an ordinary person from an ordinary family in an ordinary town. She'd taken her nothing-special education and her dime-a-dozen degree and her middlebrow tastes to Washington seeking neither wealth nor power nor fame. She'd asked for nothing more than the chance to be a tiny part of something that mattered, to toil in anonymous drudgery so that people like Jeffrey Quentin and Scott Pilkington—and Richard Michaelson—could carry saddle leather briefcases into walnut-wainscoted conference rooms and make a little history now and then.

For that, it seemed, she'd died. Her ordinary life had ended, and what was left of the ordinary lives of the ordinary people who'd brought her into the world and nurtured her and sent her to school would now be filled with grief. She'd overreached, of course, and there was nothing particularly noble about it. To impress a man—no, Michaelson corrected himself, to impress herself for a man's sake—she'd taken what she implied was hot information and basically offered it for bids. She'd put her own modest ambition above both public interest and private loyalty, at least dimly glimpsing the risks that entailed.

So all right, she wasn't Edith Cavell or Joan of Arc. She hadn't died for cause or country, she'd gone bungee jumping and the cord had snapped. But reminding himself of that didn't make Michaelson's frustration go away. Lonely death seemed too high a price to pay for misjudgment and overreaching. Sharon Bedford had died because of unreasoning self-doubt, and that was something that engaged Michaelson's gut as well as his mind.

He struggled methodically to control the unanticipated emotion. That wasn't why he was in this thing. Anger like that, he thought, was meretricious. It not only kept you from doing your job right, it made you think you were doing it better than you'd ever done it before. You thought you were looking reality right in the eyes, but instead you were gazing at it through a filter that radically distorted everything you saw. By the time Michaelson had finished these reflections, he heard Marjorie marching back into the room from the bedroom.

"Her television's in there," Marjorie announced. "Also an alarm-clock radio, an old-fashioned turntable-style record player, and some albums."

"Barry Manilow, Julio Iglesias, and John Denver," Gallagher said quietly.

"Yes. No ashtray, by the way. I haven't been able to find one in here, either."

Michaelson looked around, mildly surprised at the comment.

"Do you think that's important?" he asked.

"It confirms a comment Wendy made when I spoke to her last night," Marjorie said. "She said that when she saw Bedford at the conference having a cigarette with Quentin, she looked like she wasn't a habitual smoker—that she was just using the cigarette as a way to have Quentin to herself for a few minutes."

"I never saw her smoke the year and a half I knew her," Gallagher said, nodding. "She asked for nonsmoking sections in restaurants, and she didn't carry cigarettes with her."

"So that fits," Marjorie said.

"Well," Michaelson said, approximating a down-to-business tone, "our working theory is that if Sharon was murdered, it had something to do with the supposedly sensitive information she was shopping around the conference. Quentin probably wanted it, Pilkington certainly wanted it, others may have wanted it. So we'd like to know what that information is."

"Sounds right to me," Gallagher said.

"Before she left for the conference, she mailed off a list with several items that we can account for and an intriguing phrase, 'Highways to Indians,' that we can't. It follows that we're here to look for something that may or may not be related to that phrase. We don't know what it is or where to look for it. We can't be sure it was ever in this apartment or, if it was, that it's still here. If we happen to stumble across it, we may well not know it when we find it. Let's get to work, shall we?"

"Any hints?" Marjorie asked. "Aside from 'Highways to Indians'?"

Michaelson considered mentioning his speculation that the information had something to do with a general's relative moving to the head of the line for a rare-match liver transplant—the potential scandal that Deborah Moodie had gotten into trouble for pursuing. He decided against it. The possible connection was too conjectural to be helpful in the search they were about to start.

"Not many," he answered instead. "Ms. Bedford told Wendy and me—among others, presumably—that the information she had could be immediately useful to someone hustling for a national office or already holding one. Whatever it is, this item is presumably connected to the period from 'eighty-five to 'eighty-nine, when she was working on the staff of the national security adviser."

"Headline-worthy information, then," Marjorie said. "That's something, I suppose."

"Not just information, I don't think," Michaelson said. "When Ms. Bedford was talking to me, she mentioned *showing* something to me when we both got back to Washington. I think she was talking about tangible documentation: a letter, a memo, a picture. Something that would speak for itself, whose significance I'd instantly recognize."

"All right," Gallagher said. "Let's do it."

They did it. For the next two hours they leafed patiently through the books and manuals on Bedford's shelves, examined the space between the frame backings and the pictures and certificates on her wall, checked the ice-cube trays in her freezer and the coffee and seasoning canisters on her kitchen counter, unscrewed the numeral plate on the outside of her door on the off chance that she'd read *Casino Royale*, inspected the drains in her sinks and bathtub, probed the holding tank and drain-plug on her toilet, patted her wallpaper and the back of her vanity mirror in search of suspicious padding, looked under her mattress and sofa cushions, lifted her carpets, and rummaged through her drawers, closets, and cabinets.

They didn't find anything that looked very promising.

"Well," Michaelson said when they'd finally run out of places to search, "we had to try."

"I'll tell you one thing," Gallagher said. "We weren't the first ones to have this idea. Someone's been through this place before us."

"They must have been pretty careful about it," Michaelson said. "Why do you say that?"

"When you get to know someone pretty well, you get a feeling about the way she keeps her things arranged. I just thought to myself as I was going through this stuff, This isn't exactly the way Sharon would have left this."

"If someone else has searched the place before," Michaelson said, "he or she apparently knew how to avoid tripping the alarm, and was then cautious enough to reset it before leaving. That's not without interest."

"All that's left is the computer and the disks," Marjorie said. "I guess we might as well take a look at them."

"You're right, of course," Michaelson said. "But what we're looking for shouldn't be on either one."

"Why not?" Gallagher asked.

"Because you can't *document* a political scandal by pulling words off your own computer's hard drive or your own disks. You or I could sit down with nothing but a keyboard and our fertile imaginations and confect a paper trail implicating the president in everything from real-estate fraud to transvestite orgies, but the *Washington Post* wouldn't give us the time of day for it. It wouldn't prove anything except that we could type."

"Let's take a stab at it anyway," Marjorie said.

She flipped on the computer and the monitor. A bit too quickly for comfort, the screen flashed INITIAL 64K MEMORY ERROR. Then the screen went blank.

"Turn it off," Gallagher snapped decisively as he dug a knife from his trousers and stepped toward the unit.

With a quizzical shrug, Marjorie obeyed. Gallagher immediately began to loosen the screws on the back of the processing unit's casing.

"Are you sure that's a good idea?" Michaelson asked.

"Nope," Gallagher said, laying the first screw beside the unit and going to work on the second. "I wasn't sure it was a good idea to enlist in the army, either, and look how that turned out."

A minute and a half later, Gallagher lifted the top of the casing up.

"It looks a bit sparse," Michaelson said.

"It's missing at least two boards, even allowing for expansion slots," Gallagher said.

"So we have a computer here that's had the cybernetic equivalent of a prefrontal lobotomy?" Marjorie asked.

"That's about the size of it," Gallagher said.

"I guess someone did get here before us," Marjorie said as she gathered the handful of disks left beside the computer. After a moment's hesitation, she scooped up a manila folder holding Bedford's copies of invoices she'd sent for deposition summaries she'd prepared. Most of them were addressed to a local law firm identified as Hayes & Barthelt.

"We've accomplished one thing, even if we haven't found what we were looking for," Michaelson said. "We've established conclusively, at least to my satisfaction, that Ms. Bedford was murdered. Suicide or accident followed by a painstaking, professional search of her apartment is the kind of coincidence that just doesn't happen."

"Fair enough," Gallagher said. "But I don't see how we're much closer to knowing who killed her, and that's the next thing I plan on finding out."

"Let me suggest," Michaelson said, "that the next thing we should plan on finding out isn't who killed Ms. Bedford but why."

"If you can guarantee me that why will lead us to who, I'm game," Gallagher said.

"I can't, but I can guarantee that no other course will lead us to who, and this one might. I don't know if the murderer is at the end of this trail, but I'm certain he isn't at the end of any other one. Why is the only card that it makes any sense for us to play."

chapter

9

★

Like most soldiers, they seemed impossibly young until you looked at their eyes. The four white and two black women in the five-by-seven photograph seemed scarcely more than girls, apprentice women who might have been planning a homecoming dance, their khaki uniforms jarringly incongruous. Then you caught their eyes, and that changed everything.

"Six nurses in that picture and four of us have cigarettes," Deborah Moodie said in a can-you-believe-it tone, as if the demonization of tobacco were the biggest change in the country since 1968. "I got rid of mine just before they snapped the shot. I was afraid my mama might see the picture someday."

"A more innocent time in a lot of ways, I suppose," Michaelson said, leaning forward to look more closely at the photograph. It was Sunday night and he was basking in the relaxed comfort of the Moodies' Montgomery Park home. He'd called Alex Moodie immediately after Gallagher had dropped him off. Asking for a brief visit, he'd found himself invited over immediately for drinks.

"It wasn't innocence, it was 'Nam," said the still slender black woman whose hair was now touched with gray. "If you'd told us we were going to die of cancer in forty years, we'd have said, 'I'll take it.' Especially after Tet, we weren't any of us betting we had the next forty days guaranteed, much less forty years."

Alex Moodie approached, carrying a tray with three glasses of scotch and a soda spritzer. Michaelson and Deborah Moodie each took a glass. It was a tiny act of generational complicity, a taste that Michaelson and the Moodies shared with one another but not with those around Wendy Gardner's and Sharon Bedford's ages.

"I've brought you only bad news so far," Michaelson said.

"It was news I had to have, though," Deborah Moodie said. "And I know it wasn't easy."

"I have more. Scott Pilkington has asked me to do something for him. I agreed on several conditions, one of them being cover for you. His response was equivocal."

"Why would I need cover?"

"Because I want the name of the general who got favored treatment in the incident you were pursuing," Michaelson said.

"And you can't get that from anyone but me?" A challenging glint brightened Deborah Moodie's eyes as she asked the question. That query came from the Potomac, not the Mekong Delta.

"I don't know," Michaelson answered. "But regardless of whom I get it from, Pilkington will assume I got it from you. That's why you need cover."

"Thanks for asking, then. Why do you need that name?"

"It's a long story."

"There's plenty of scotch," Alex Moodie said.

"Very well," Michaelson said. "On the Sunday of the Contemporary Policy Dynamics Conference in West Virginia, a woman named Sharon Bedford died. I'm convinced she was murdered. Before dying she'd hinted to me and probably to several others that she had sensitive information."

"But she didn't say what it was," Deborah Moodie guessed.

"Right. She was making these hints as part of a job search."

"Pilkington was there and she probably shopped the information to him, too," Alex Moodie said.

"Right again. Put that together with Pilkington jumping through hoops to set our meeting up at the CPD Conference instead of at a cocktail lounge in Washington, and what do you get?"

"Speculation," Deborah Moodie said. "One possibility is that what Pilkington was really interested in even before the conference was Bedford's hints, and he met with you and Alex as a diversion."

"Agreed," Michaelson said. "A related possibility is that Pilkington thought Bedford's information might be connected somehow to the topic of his meeting with Alex and me."

"Which is why you need the general's name," Alex Moodie said.

"Walt Artemus," Deborah Moodie said. "Retired major general."

"That name doesn't ring much of a bell," Michaelson said.

"No particular reason it should. He wasn't political and he didn't have a very high profile outside the Pentagon. He only got his second star as a retirement present. His last long-term posting was military aide on the White House staff."

"Working with the national security adviser?" Michaelson asked, his interest sharply piqued.

"No," Deborah said, shaking her head emphatically. "That's the first thing I thought, too, but according to Alex's sources, he reported directly to the president's chief of staff and not to the national security adviser."

"That seems odd," Michaelson muttered, but he decided to think through the implications later. He looked directly at Deborah. "As to your role in the underlying incident itself, what I have so far is Pilkington's version. I'd like to hear yours."

Shrugging, Deborah Moodie walked away from the bookshelf and found a place on a sofa against the opposite wall. Michaelson read unmistakable pain in her eyes as she dredged up the memory.

"Pilkington's version isn't that far off, if you look at it his way," she began. "It started in mid- to late 'ninety. I was supposed to sign off on an option paper about different ways to ration medical services, if we ever stop just selling them to the highest bidder. I'm translating it into plain English for you, you understand. The paper itself didn't actually come out and admit that rationing was what it was talking about."

"I shouldn't think so."

"Anyway, it was a pretty standard-issue Washington work product. The executive summary was one page long, the body of the paper was thirty-two pages, and then eighty pages of appendices were attached. An appendix is always the safest place to put the truth in a report like that, so that's where I looked for it."

"And the truth turned out to be what?" Michaelson prompted.

"The truth turned out not to be there. I studied the appendix summarizing the sets of standards used to decide who gets organ transplants, because that's the one area where we haven't been able to kid ourselves about rationing. We've faced up to it because we haven't had any choice: it's triage, someone's gonna live and someone's gonna die, and we have to decide who.

"This appendix included a table, and the column for liver transplants had a footnote that said, 'Data incomplete because of extra-criterial allocations.'"

"Meaning what?"

"That's what I intended to find out. Turns out it meant that some liver transplants went to people who got pushed to the top of the list without reference to the triage criteria. I asked for summaries of every case where that had happened. The name of Walt Artemus's daughter came up, and my antennae started quivering big time. That's what I meant when I said Pilkington wasn't that far off. I thought maybe I was really onto something. I'll admit it: I really did see myself testifying in front of a congressional committee and being interviewed on CNN and PBS."

"So. What did you do?" Michaelson asked.

"Just what Pilkington said I should've done," Deborah said. "I wrote my own report with my own executive summary and a snappy little action memo attached to it."

"And nothing happened."

"Right. Tickled it after one month, tickled it after three months, six months, nine months. Nothing."

"So you pushed."

"Not right away, to tell you the truth," Deborah said. "I'd do a little follow-up memo every few months, just to sort of stake my claim to the issue. The kind of thing that goes from the in-basket to the out-basket with eight-point-two seconds' reading time in between. But I didn't start breaking furniture until early 'ninety-three. That's what got me taken to the woodshed."

"What did you start doing then?"

"Went outside channels. I even went outside the service. Started adding bitchy little cc's to the memos. And then," Deborah added, suddenly lowering her voice at the enormity of what she was about to confess, "I threatened to go to the Hill."

Michaelson did his best to look shocked. The executive branch mentality knows no heresy more outrageous than the notion that the elected representatives of the people should be allowed to participate in governing the country.

"What provoked you to this, ah, extreme measure?" Michaelson asked carefully.

"It just started to get to me," Deborah explained, her tone rising slightly in angry frustration. "I wasn't always a suit. I didn't learn about triage from thirty-page reports, I learned about it in an OR at Da Nang."

She leaned forward, eyes widening with intensity as her face came alive.

"The triage rules at Da Nang were crystal clear, especially during Tet. The marines we treated first weren't the ones about to die or the ones in the most pain. They were the ones who could be patched up quickest and sent back to kill more Charlie."

"Yes," Michaelson said softly, "I do see."

"So I'm sitting at my desk in 1993 and we're not under fire, we don't have a defense perimeter to worry about, and we don't have bodybags piling up like cordwood. Yet some lifer with a charity star and a Rolodex is making up his own little triage rules, and someone *dies* because of it. It just got to me."

Settling back, Michaelson took a sip of scotch. The sip turned into a substantial swallow. Gazing steadily at the mildly abashed smile that split Deborah Moodie's lips, he thought for a moment about which of the two lies he should call her on. He chose the first.

"Your description of how you got caught up in this issue in the first place was very thorough," he said.

"Thank you."

"As you went through it, though, the mischievous notion occurred to me that, somewhere along the line at the beginning there, someone might have given you a hint."

Deborah's face went flat. Michaelson imagined an armored knight flipping down the visor on his helmet: one instant you saw a human face, and the next you saw nothing but cold steel and angry eyes.

"Did you have any particular source for that hint in mind?" she asked in a taut voice.

"I was hoping you'd tell me."

"I thought I just did tell you."

Michaelson rested his forearms on his knees. He did his best to open his own features up, to disguise the threat implicit in his dark, piercing eyes.

"I've worked with cover stories for over forty years," he said mildly. "I know one when I hear one."

"That's out of line," Alex Moodie snapped in a low tone that tried to match Michaelson's and didn't quite make it. He moved a couple of protective steps closer to his wife.

"We've been sparring for close to a minute now and Deborah hasn't told me I'm wrong," Michaelson said. "If I'm out of line, I'd like to hear it from her."

"Do you really think I made all that stuff up about the report and the table in the appendix?" she asked.

"No, I don't. I think you just started somewhere after the beginning. And I still haven't heard you tell me I'm wrong."

Deborah lifted her glass and drank briefly. The sip was measured, practiced, calculated sedulously to suggest that the liquor was appreciated but not needed.

"You're not wrong," she said. "Someone did leak some sketchy information about the incident to me, and I dug the report out to start following it up."

"And to cover the leak," Michaelson suggested, nodding.

"True," Deborah said, a bit pointedly for someone who'd been on the defensive five seconds before. "When someone's done you a favor, you don't want to leave them hanging out to dry."

"Absolutely right. Of course, you wouldn't be hanging Sharon Bedford out to dry at this point, would you?"

"You're right," Deborah said as she finished her scotch and soda. "She doesn't have anything to fear now from any bureaucrat in the world."

chapter

10

★

I'm glad that one of us had a productive evening," Marjorie said around eleven o'clock Monday morning, after Michaelson had summarized his Sunday-night talk with the Moodies. "If it was Bedford who gave Deborah Moodie the story about this general getting favorable treatment on a transplant, then that has to be related somehow to whatever Bedford was shopping around at the CPD conference."

"Implying that Pilkington's chat with Alex and me and his interest in Bedford's death isn't exactly a coincidence, either," Michaelson said.

"Right."

They were in the backroom of Cavalier Books, Marjorie's store just beyond Dupont Circle on Connecticut Avenue. Marjorie was in the process of returning three dozen hardcover books to their respectable but soon to be poorer publisher.

"Nothing useful on the disks you took from her apartment?" Michaelson guessed.

"Nothing. They're bootleg copies of games. If a tantalizing clue is hidden somewhere within them, I didn't stumble across it."

"We may have another shot on the computer disk front. I phoned Scott Pilkington first thing this morning."

"You mean you left a message for him around nine and he returned your call before lunch?" Marjorie asked, her voice pitching upward in astonishment that was only partially feigned.

"He actually answered when I called. On the second ring."

"You must feel drunk with power."

"I very nearly called a press conference."

"What did he tell you about computer disks?" Marjorie asked.

"That the police didn't find any in Ms. Bedford's hotel room, even though she had a laptop computer with her."

"That doesn't sound very promising," Marjorie said. After packing two last handfuls of books into a cardboard box, she closed the flaps and expertly taped them shut.

"The promising part is that the laptop itself wasn't stripped of its hard drive, as the computer in her apartment was. Pilkington has persuaded the police to let one of his functionaries pop down and copy everything on it. If Federal Express performs with its customary efficiency, he'll have the data by noon tomorrow."

"That's curious," Marjorie said. "Why would the murderer leave one computer alone and then gut the other one?"

"One intriguing possibility is that the murderer isn't the one who searched her apartment—that the murderer knew what he was looking for in the hotel room, and whoever searched her apartment didn't. Another plausible explanation is that the murderer wasn't trying to find something but to keep someone else from finding something."

"Something that police in Charleston wouldn't have any

reason to look for, but that someone in Washington would," Marjorie said, her eyes brightening at the idea's plausibility.

"That was my thought," Michaelson said.

"Promise you'll show me the disks when they come in tomorrow."

"If I can extract them from Pilkington, I certainly shall."

"Is there some doubt about that?" Marjorie asked. "I thought he was eager to keep you happy so that you'd keep on coopting Gallagher."

"That's not exactly a pat hand. If he decides I'm overplaying it, he'll send me on my way with one of his little Princeton eating club *mots*, and I'll be about as much use as those bootleg game disks left in Ms. Bedford's apartment."

"You never were exactly an optimist, were you?" Marjorie commented.

"Optimism is a luxury purchased with ignorance. I've never been able to afford it."

"Speaking of eating club *mots*."

"It's contagious, isn't it?" Michaelson said, half-apologetically. "I spend twenty minutes on the phone with him and he has me doing it."

The phone on Marjorie's desk burred with polite insistence. She glanced at a tiny screen near the receiver, where she could read the number the call came from.

"That will be Susanna Herro calling back," she said, reaching for the receiver.

"Who's she?" Michaelson asked.

"An attorney wise in the ways of law firm organization."

"I'll check back with you this evening," Michaelson said, standing and moving toward the door. "Something tells me I'll have a better shot at the disks if I've found out what

General Walt Artemus's White House job was before I talk to Pilkington again."

Nodding her farewell to Michaelson, Marjorie greeted Herro on the phone.

"I hope you're calling to tell me that an exciting new legal thriller will be coming out soon," Herro said. "Several of the partners here read them when they feel like escaping from the tedium of real-world law practice."

"I have my eyes open for one," Marjorie said, "but I'm calling now to get information rather than dispense it."

"What would you like to know?"

"I want to talk to someone at a local Bethesda law firm called Hayes and Barthelt about a woman who did freelance deposition summaries for them. Whom should I ask for?"

"If the firm has more than twenty lawyers, ask for the head paralegal," Herro said.

"What if it has fewer than twenty lawyers?"

"Then it doesn't have any business using freelancers to summarize depositions."

"Thank you again," Marjorie said. "I'll let you know the instant I spot the next female Perry Mason."

★

Michaelson's preference for print on paper over pixels on video screens verged on superstition. There were a lot of ways he could have gotten a look at *T/O: The United States Armed Forces Directory*, and the simplest would have been to punch some buttons on the computer that dominated a credenza behind his desk at the Brookings Institution. He chose instead to go to the Library of Congress, where he could secure a hard copy of the bulky tome and lug it to a desk in the reading room. Something about physically flipping through bound paper and looking at an entire page of text at a time seemed to stimulate thought in ways that electronic dots and screen scrolls didn't.

It took him until well into the afternoon to learn that Walter Page Artemus had been commissioned as a second lieutenant in the United States Army after graduating third in his class at West Point in 1964. He had served three tours in Vietnam, receiving one citation for extraordinary valor displayed during the chaotic fighting that dominated the first two days of the Tet offensive. Emerging from the post-Vietnam military reorganization as a lieutenant-colonel, he had made full colonel in 1981 and become a brigadier general in 1985. His postings along the way had included a line command at Fort Bragg, a stint in "Procurement/Weapons and Weapons Systems (Major)" at the Pentagon, and a staff position at NATO headquarters in Brussels.

The promotion to brigadier had coincided with Artemus's assignment to the White House staff as a military aide. Duties otherwise unspecified. He had served in that capacity throughout President Reagan's second term. Then he had crossed the Potomac again, returning to the Pentagon to head a working group at POLF—Planning and Operations, Land Forces. This, however, had continued only until the summer of 1990, when he received a promotion to major general and almost simultaneously retired.

Retired. Under fifty.

Early retirement happened in the army, especially to flag officers who'd bumped against the ceiling in the course of the armed services' relentless up-or-out promotion system. Michaelson had seen the same thing happen to colleagues of his own under the equivalent winnowing process that prevailed in the foreign service. But retirement before fifty of someone with a record as solid as the one Artemus had built struck Michaelson as extraordinary.

A few months after Artemus retired, Michaelson noted thoughtfully, the United States was hip-deep in its biggest shooting war since Vietnam and was mobilizing reservists from New Jersey to Newport Beach. But if the entry before him was up to date, it apparently hadn't occurred to anyone to ask General Walter P. Artemus (Ret.) to jump back in and lend a hand for the duration. That, if nothing else, suggested to Michaelson that Deborah Moodie had been right about Artemus's last promotion: a going-away present to sweeten the pension, a charity star on the way out the door.

Michaelson wasn't sure as he cabbed back to Brookings

whether to call Jeffrey Quentin or Scott Pilkington. He knew more about Artemus than he'd expected to at this stage, but he still had only an informed suspicion about what Artemus's actual job on the White House staff had been.

He hadn't resolved the issue by the time he was back at his desk, so he called Todd Gallagher instead. Gallagher came on the line with an alacrity suggesting that whatever he was working on had a lower priority than anything Michaelson might have to tell him.

Michaelson began by describing his meeting with the Moodies. He went over it in detail, not only replaying the conversation but trying to recapture the scene, the feeling, and intensity in the room.

"That stuff about why she picked the issue back up and escalated the attack in 'ninety-three doesn't ring true, somehow," Gallagher said.

"I think it's true, I just don't think it's complete," Michaelson said.

"It seems too pat."

"If you'd seen the picture she still has displayed from her Vietnam days, you wouldn't doubt her sincerity on that score," Michaelson said.

He described the photograph in detail—the eyes, the uniforms, the cigarettes, the faces, and the poses of the young nurses—trying to make Gallagher understand what had to be the searing intensity of Deborah Moodie's experience in Vietnam.

"Maybe so," Gallagher said soberly when he'd finished. "Maybe we don't have all of it, but maybe what we have is true. What else you got?"

Michaelson quickly summarized Artemus's service record,

venturing the assessment that it seemed rather impressive.

"Chicken colonel less than eighteen years out of the Point?" Gallagher exclaimed. "That's not impressive, that's walking on water. The absolute statutory minimum is thirteen and a half years, and we'd have to have an awful bloody damn war before anyone could even think about getting his eagle that fast. He must've made at least two grades below zone."

"What does that mean?"

"Before he'd served the normal time in rank."

"The citation might have given him a boost on one of them," Michaelson suggested.

"Actually, one of the most impressive things to me in his whole record is that he only picked up one medal in three tours. Lifers from the Point got tin thrown at them with both hands. Junior officers out of ROTC like yours truly didn't worry too much about that kind of thing. Being too eager for a medal could get you fragged, for one thing."

Michaelson closed his eyes at that grating word from the bitter, late-war era. "Fragged" meant having a hand grenade thrown into your tent by one of your own men.

"So if he was only cited for bravery once, that tells you he wasn't playing army politics in Vietnam?" Michaelson asked.

"That's right. Not just dropping in to get his ticket punched, and not using his men as chips in that cozy little poker game the Pointers had going among themselves over there."

"His retirement seems a bit abrupt, especially against that background," Michaelson said.

"If they thought he was anywhere near retiring, they wouldn't have sent him to POLF after he was through having his picture taken at the White House," Gallagher said. "POLF is heavy-duty, big-time brass-hat action. Short of a combat command in an honest-to-God bombs-and-bullets scrap some-where, it's about the best assignment someone in his position could have hoped for."

"Thank you," Michaelson said distractedly as he followed a train of thought that Gallagher's comment had started. "I'll get in touch again as soon as there's another development."

His eagerness to follow up a provocative lead quickly pre-empting his preference for print, Michaelson flipped his com-puter on as soon as he'd hung up. He pushed the buttons required to summon the *Washington Post*'s style and magazine sections to his screen. As Gallagher's offhand crack suggested, people who serve at the White House do tend to get their pictures taken. If that had happened to Artemus—and it should have—the photo ought to have shown up in one of the two places he was looking.

It didn't. That was when Michaelson decided to call Quen-tin instead of Pilkington.

It took him an hour to get a call back from the assistant to Quentin's secretary. She explained that Mr. Quentin's sched-ule was quite full and that an appointment anytime that week was out of the question.

"Would you mind very much putting in your message to Mr. Quentin that the subject of my proposed conversation is General Artemus, and that I think the topic is time-critical?"

"Certainly. If Mr. Quentin agrees, I'm sure he'll have me get back to you."

"I'll be here all afternoon," Michaelson said.

★

When Marjorie showed up for her three P.M. appointment with Leslie Davidson, the head paralegal at Hayes & Barthelt, she assumed that she'd be meeting a woman. She was surprised when a cherubic male wearing a bright red vest underneath a blue sport coat toddled out to greet her. He smiled from beneath a luxurious gray mustache as he shook hands with her.

"Fair warning," he said. He pointed toward the wall at an elegant brass plaque with a black circle/slash over a lighted cigarette, subscribed with the prohibition SMOKING FORBIDDEN. "The sign in my office is very different."

"I'm on notice," Marjorie acknowledged as she followed him out of the reception area and down the hall.

They passed a frosted glass door marked LOUNGE. The plaque on that door had the circle and the cigarette without the slash and proclaimed, SMOKING PERMITTED. A left turn brought them to a small internal office with a cozy secretarial area outside it. A handmade cardboard parody of the earlier plaques showed a circle around an open lighter displaying a steady flame. The words underneath were SMOKING ENCOURAGED.

Finally, they stepped into Davidson's office. The cardboard plaque there showed an open pack of cigarettes inside its circle and sternly enjoined, SMOKING COMPULSORY. Complementing the message was a sign beside the ashtray on Davidson's desk: THANK YOU FOR MINDING YOUR OWN BUSINESS. The distinctive smell and taste of the room—for it had both— brought memories of the senior lounge at college flooding back to Marjorie. She was considering an allusion to Proust's madeleine when Davidson lit a Vantage and spun the pack across the desk toward her.

"No, thank you," said Marjorie, who preferred a somewhat less fanatical ambience for the two dozen or so cigarettes she still consumed each year. "I think that actually having one in my mouth would be superfluous."

"Sharon Bedford," Davidson said then, settling into the amply cushioned chair behind his el-shaped desk. "Good kid. That's really why I agreed to talk to you. I don't want to let go of her. When I heard she was dead, I felt like someone had punched me in the stomach. Left me feeling empty, you know?"

"Yes," Marjorie said.

"Sharon was top notch at what she did. She could have been a real paralegal if she'd wanted to be, and she might have become absolutely world-class."

" 'Could have been'?" Marjorie asked.

"She wasn't a paralegal when she died, she was only a deposition summary freelancer," Davidson said, raising an index finger to emphasize the fine point.

"What's the difference?"

"A deposition summary freelancer is what it sounds like. A paralegal is somewhere between a glorified secretary and a frustrated lawyer. A paralegal does a lot more than summarize depositions."

"So Sharon had a very narrow specialty but excelled at it," Marjorie prompted.

"Deposition summaries are an art form and hers were beautiful," Davidson said with a dreamy glance at the ceiling, like an old Washington Senators fan remembering Camilo Pascual's curveball. "She'd capsulize six pages in four lines, I'd check it over, and there wouldn't be one important fact left out. Then she'd take three-quarters of a summary page to cover two transcript pages, I'd check it, and there wouldn't be a word I could delete."

"I guess she was a smart girl," Marjorie said.

"You bet. I kept trying to talk her into other things: indexing documents, drafting simple pleadings, checking court records, interviewing witnesses—you know, halfway interesting stuff. No go. She didn't want to do anything but summarize deps. She wouldn't let me move her up in the profession."

"I didn't realize paralegals could entertain such a broad range of career aspirations."

"Are you kidding?" Davidson demanded. "Ninety percent of what paralegals do is stuff that lawyers did twenty-five years ago. It doesn't take a Harvard graduate to pull a removal petition out of the form file and fill in the blanks. These days they even have us doing basic legal research. We work a lot cheaper than young lawyers, and they never have to make us partners."

The tincture of bitterness coloring the last sentence suggested to Marjorie that a new topic might be in order.

"Did any of the depositions that Sharon worked on involve unusually sensitive matters?"

"Nah," Davidson said dismissively as he brushed tobacco flakes from his lapel. "This is your basic bread-and-butter practice: the machine didn't work, the broker churned Aunt Millie's account, the supplier cut off my dealership contract without good cause. You're never going to see a case from this firm on the front page of the *Post*."

"Would it be possible for information in one of your cases to have serious implications for something really important—or someone really important—that wasn't directly involved in the case?"

"Sure, in theory. But it'd be hard for anything to be a state secret by the time it got to Sharon. Before it can be in a deposition, a witness has to know it and then he has to say it. As soon as he says it, at least two lawyers and a court reporter hear it. We're not talking about the Pentagon Papers here."

Marjorie paused for a moment in frustration. She found these answers extremely inconvenient and aggravatingly plausible.

"Look," Davidson said, "I know where you're going with this. I had the same reaction when I heard about Sharon dying alone in a hotel room: 'I don't want this to be suicide, and I don't want it to be some kind of a screwed-up drug deal gone bad.' I mean, she was just too neat a person to die like that. If she has to be dead, I at least want there to be something significant about her death."

"Exactly," Marjorie said.

"But it just ain't there," Davidson said, turning to face her head on and planting his elbows on his desk, his face a picture of earnest resignation. "At least from this end. You just can't get there from here."

Before she could answer, Marjorie became aware of someone waiting none too patiently in the doorway behind her.

"Sorry to interrupt, Les," a young male voice said in a tone which made it clear that the apology was strictly *pro forma*, "but I need something quick and half the office is in court or at a closing."

"Shoot," Davidson said.

"Under Indiana choice of law rules, what state's law governs the effectiveness of a written-amendments-only clause in a non-exclusive dealership contract?"

"Code-governed?"

"Assume no."

"Got it," Davidson said.

"I need the answer before the night help comes on at six."

"You'll have it in forty-five minutes."

"Great. Thanks."

"I can see you're going to be busy," Marjorie said. She began to gather her purse up as Davidson opened the top drawer of his desk and fumbled in it.

"Nah, gimme ten minutes," he said. "I enjoy talking about Sharon, and I'm not going to stop just because some kid's too important to do his own grunt work. Now, where did I put the damn thing?"

Marjorie waited uncertainly as Davidson closed the drawer and laboriously pulled a Samsonite attaché case onto the desk.

"Here it is," he said triumphantly, pulling a single sheet of white, printed, legal-sized paper from it. "Sharon gave me that," he added, pointing to a small, oblong silver plate with black lettering that decorated the front of the attaché case's lid.

" '*Illegitimi Non Carborundum*,' " Marjorie read as Davidson flattened the sheet beside his computer and began massaging the keyboard. " 'Don't let the bastards get you down.' "

"You know Latin, huh?" Davidson asked absently. He was now seated in profile and mostly hidden by the open attaché case as he faced his computer screen.

"*Proculdubior*," Marjorie said. "So did Sharon, apparently."

Concentrating on the screen, Davidson offered only a non-committal grunt in response. Several minutes passed, punctuated by intermittent commentary from Davidson, who seemed eager to keep the interruption from weighing too heavily on his guest.

"Used to be you did research in books. . . . Probably before the kid's time. . . . Tell ya, there was a time a lawyer would've cut his arm off before he had a civilian find a case for him. . . .

Bingo. Got it. Now I'll E-mail it to the kid and see if he can get the case into his brief without someone holding his hand while he does it."

Davidson flipped the attaché case closed and folded his hands complacently on top of it, laughing a little at his own self-satisfaction.

"Do you mean that in the last five minutes or so you found a case answering the obscure question that lawyer just asked you?"

"Yep."

He paused for a moment, grinning ambiguously like a conjurer who's made an elephant disappear and can't decide whether to reveal the cleverness of his trick or maintain the illusion of his magic. Cleverness won.

"It's not that big a deal, actually," he said, holding up the sheet he'd taken from his attaché case. "For ten decades or so, the West Publishing Company has divided all of American law into four hundred and twelve subjects, from Abatement and Revival to Zoning and Planning. They've divided each subject into topics and subtopics, from twelve topics for Dueling to over a thousand for subjects like Appeal and Error and Federal Civil Procedure. They've given every topic a number."

"That sounds pretty daunting."

"Now that we're on computers," Davidson continued, "there's also a special code number for every subject. That's what's listed on this sheet. So you just go into the WestLaw database, ask for Indiana cases, code number 94 for Contracts, topic number 144 for Law Governing, and look at the most recent case. If it makes sense, you've answered the question."

"It's too bad they'll never make you a partner."

"Yeah, it is," Davidson agreed. "But that's a decision I made more than thirty years ago. Anyway, you came here to talk about Sharon Bedford, not me, and I don't think you were finished yet."

"I was just wondering as I thought about what you said. Just play Let's Pretend with me for a second. Say Sharon picked up some isolated bit of information in one of the depositions she was reviewing—something that meant nothing special to the lawyers and the parties. Let's say, though, that because of something else she knew, from her own background, she realized that information was actually very important. Big-league stuff. Possible?"

"Again, you say 'possible' and again I guess anything's *possible*. I'd love for it to be true. Tell you the truth, I just don't see it. I'll tell you one thing for damn sure, though. If she did stumble on something, she made a record of it. She was absolutely the most meticulous person I've ever met. If God needs a staff clerk, He's got one now."

"Made a record of it somewhere in a deposition summary, do you think?"

"If she did and you can find it," Davidson said with a smile and an exasperated shrug, "you're a better man than I am. 'Cause I'll tell you something: I've looked, and I don't think it's there."

"Mr. Michaelson?" the feminine voice chirped at 5:17, when Michaelson was just about to give up. "Please hold for Mr. Quentin."

Michaelson held while he tried to decide whether this ap-

proach reflected simple insensitivity or calculated rudeness.
After holding for one hundred and seventy irritating seconds,
he decided that he didn't care. Then Quentin came on the
line.

"Show me some tit," were the first words out of his mouth.

"I beg your pardon?" asked Michaelson in unfeigned bafflement.

"The tease is cute, but I don't have time for finger-
fucking," Quentin replied. "If it's falsies under the D-cups,
you don't get my room key."

"Fair enough," said Michaelson, as something like understanding dawned. "Here goes. For twenty-five years-
plus Walter Page Artemus soared through a dazzling army
career. Late in the twenty-sixth, at the precise moment
when he'd put his foot on the first step of the last stairway
to the top, he inexplicably retired. He had 'chief of staff'
written all over his ticket, then he crashed and burned overnight."

"Everyone in town who can read knows that." Quentin
yawned. "Everyone who cares, anyway."

"What everyone in town doesn't know is why—and it's not
because he abused his rank to get special treatment for a
relative."

"So. Tell me why."

"Not over the phone," Michaelson said.

"Translation: You don't know why, either."

"That depends on how you define 'know.' In any event,
I'm confident that between the two of us we could find out for
sure. And I think that's something you haven't been able to do
all by yourself up to now."

"I ask for tit and you're blowing goddamn smoke up my

ass," Quentin said. "Show me you have something besides bullshit in your sample case or this phone call is
over."

"I understand," Michaelson said apologetically. "I've been
out of the game for a while, and my reflexes are a bit rusty.
Need not to know and so forth. Scott Pilkington is running on
this one, and I'm supposed to talk to him."

Michaelson winced as he finished this comment, anticipat-
ing an angry, contemptuous *click* It didn't come. When Quentin spoke again after two seconds of suspenseful silence, he
had dropped the bullying swagger from his voice, in favor of
aw-shucks innocence.

"Who's Scott Pilkington?" he asked.

"Whose Scott Pilkington?" Michaelson answered, match-
ing Quentin's tone note-for-note. "Why, your Scott Pilkington, Mr. Quentin. I didn't know anyone else owned a piece of
him."

The pause this time lasted less than one second.

"I'll have to move some things around, but I can give you
twenty minutes," Quentin snapped then. "Ten-thirty sharp
tonight."

The line went dead.

chapter

12

★

If the secular liturgy of American politics offers anything else
with the sacramental resonance of the White House at night,
Michaelson reflected, he couldn't imagine what it might be.
TV screens showing the West Wing bathed in light meant
drama, crisis, war. Michaelson had seen it before but, he
mused as the guard checked his name on a list and waved him
through at 10:23 P.M., you never stop being impressed.

Quentin's office was on the second floor of the Old Executive Office Building, directly across West Executive Avenue
from the White House. Though Quentin had occupied the
office for over three years, it looked as if he had just moved
into it and didn't expect to remain for more than a week or so.
No pictures or mementos graced the spare shelves or the dark
wood, government-issue desk. No plants competed for space
with the newspapers, magazines, videotapes, and computer
printouts covering the desk and cabinet tops. The oatmeal-
colored drapes and carpet were whatever the GSA had tossed
into the room. The only thing in the office that Quentin
seemed to have chosen was an elaborate phone console next
to his computer.

As a young woman silently ushered Michaelson into the office, Quentin stood facing the far corner, as far behind his desk as he could get. A Rorschach splotch of sweat stained the back of his powder blue shirt. With the scratch of Michaelson's chair on the floor, Quentin turned his head a fraction of an inch, showing Michaelson a sliver of his face.

"All right," he said. "Impress me."

"Artemus never had his picture taken," Michaelson said. "Four years in the Reagan White House, surrounded by lens-seeking flacks, and he didn't make it to a single photo-op."

"So what?"

"If you're trying to let me know how small a blip I am on your radar screen, that's perfect," Michaelson said. "If you're trying to make me think you really don't appreciate the significance of what I said, you're a beat too slow."

Hands snaking into his hip pockets, Quentin swiveled around.

"I *know* what I know. What you *think* I know I could give a shit. You haven't impressed me yet, and I'm beginning to think you're bluffing."

"The story of my life. Very well. I'll spell it out. Camera shy implies security conscious. Security conscious plus military aide in the White House equals football. General Artemus followed the president around with the briefcase holding the nuclear launch codes—known colloquially as the football. Armageddon in calfskin."

Quentin offered a half-smile.

"Pete Fiske carried the football for Reagan," he said in a mildly puzzled voice. "I knew that clear back when I was designing ad campaigns for dandelion killer in Marin County."

"General Fiske carried a decoy," Michaelson said, unruffled. "General Fiske wore a uniform, and General Fiske got his picture in the paper. If the Soviets happened to have a marksman in range when the flag dropped, General Fiske was supposed to catch the bullet and General Artemus was supposed to open his briefcase. Please note my polite restraint in omitting any observation about everyone in town knowing that."

"Everyone in town didn't know that," Quentin said, grinning with a hint of real warmth as he strolled back toward his desk. "How do you?"

"You wouldn't believe me if I told you, so why don't we just skip it and talk about something else? Like why General Artemus started drawing his pension fifteen years early."

"If I had that answer," Quentin said, "I wouldn't be talking to you."

"I know how frustrating it must be. You poke your nose into filing cabinets and peek under desk blotters every chance you get and you keep coming up empty."

"It hasn't exactly been my only project. But it would just about be yours, wouldn't it?"

"For all practical purposes," Michaelson conceded affably. "Of course, I'll be looking for the answer from outside the White House."

"But from inside the establishment. That's the key. I might get my face on talk shows every Sunday morning, and everybody might know I talk to the president for at least half an hour every day, but I'll always be an outsider here. So will the president himself, for that matter. I'd have a better chance of being admitted to the Players Club in London than to that chummy little group where you've spent your adult life."

"It's nice to feel needed."

"That's why you're sitting here," Quentin said. He

dropped into his chair and leaned back, reaching out idly with his left hand to tap a pencil eraser on his desktop. "Listen to me. Carefully. What you want. It's within your grasp. It is literally within your grasp. Am I coming through?"

"Quite clearly."

Quentin swiveled the chair slightly and leaned his head back, gazing at Michaelson from half-closed eyes. From the beginning of the interview his movements had seemed to Michaelson not just unnatural but elaborately choreographed, as if he'd spent ten minutes before Michaelson came in working out when to strike one pose and when to take another.

"I'm not talking about just getting a nice title to close your copybook with while a lame-duck administration plays out the string. I'm talking about an entire term. Maybe two full terms."

Quentin's eyes snapped open and he surged forward in the chair with a fierce intensity.

"Don't laugh," he said to Michaelson, who wasn't laughing. "I can do it. I can *fucking do it*. I can pull off a bigger win than Johnson in 'sixty-four. I can lock the party into the White House for years. And if you're the one who produces what I need to bring it off, you just name your price and I will, by God, deliver."

"We understand each other perfectly," Michaelson said.

"I don't just need an answer. Oliver Stone has all the answers, but he also has slightly less credibility than the Flat Earth Society. I need documentation. Hard copy. Can you get it?"

"I'd tell you yes regardless of what the truth was and you know it," Michaelson said. "So why bother to ask the question?"

For the first time in the conversation Quentin's face lit with an expression that didn't seem entirely rehearsed. His lips split in a broad grin, simultaneously malicious and delighted.

"You are a very dangerous man," he said.

"Yes I am," Michaelson said as he rose and extended his hand.

It was the first time in the last five minutes that either of them had told the complete truth.

chapter
13

★

"Wasn't Pilkington upset about you going to Quentin behind his back?" Marjorie asked when Michaelson joined her at Cavalier Books shortly before noon the next day.

"He was quite cross," Michaelson acknowledged. "At least he pretended to be. I pointed out that if I'd talked to him ahead of time, he would technically have been collaborating with me. I opined that Quentin would have seen through me instantly and tumbled to my guilty association with Pilkington, to Pilkington's presumed prejudice. At that point he pretended to be mollified."

"Did he give you the disks?"

"Disk," Michaelson said, handing a manila envelope to her. "There's only one, and I'm afraid his giving it to me means he's had someone look at it and he doesn't think there's anything significant on it."

"No sense booting it up and plugging 'Highways to Indians' into Word Search, then?" Marjorie asked.

"You know," Michaelson said thoughtfully, "I think that in the two chats I've had with Scott Pilkington since we visited Ms. Bedford's apartment, 'Highways to Indians' has somehow failed to come up in the conversation. Forgetful of me, but then I'm getting to an age where that kind of thing is apt to happen."

"I'll give the disk a try, then—even though it's a little hard to believe that I'll stumble onto something that the professionals available to Pilkington and Quentin would miss."

"Don't sell yourself short. Whatever professionals they're using haven't produced what Quentin's after yet. Partly I think that's because Quentin's not going to let anyone know exactly what he is after until he's holding it in his hand and is ready to use it. That's why he swore to me that he didn't know why General Artemus had been forced into early retirement."

"You think he was lying about that?" Marjorie asked.

"Not a doubt in my mind. He knows every detail. Sitting where he has been since the last inauguration, he'd have to be brain-dead not to learn that much if he really wanted to find it out."

"Then why did he favor you with that high-wattage sales job, that luminous bribe about naming your own cabinet position? What does he want from you?"

"He wants me to come up with usable, concrete documentation of what he already knows. He thinks there's at least a chance that I can do that. The catch is that to have a prayer of accomplishing anything like that, either you have to find a road map on the disk that will lead us to the documentation, or I have to find out why Artemus got canned and work backwards from there."

"But Quentin won't tell you why Artemus got fired, or even admit that he knows himself. So how do you plan to get the information?"

"The only idea I've come up with so far," Michaelson said without a trace of enthusiasm, "is to ask Artemus."

Michaelson took his leave and Marjorie prepared to confront the lunch-hour rush at Cavalier Books. At the stroke of two she mentally declared the rush over and hustled the computer disk Michaelson had left with her back to her Spartan desk in the stockroom.

In impatient anticipation she slipped it into her Compaq and summoned its directory onto the screen:

Ailiss v. Hardacher	PTFDEPSUM
Arliss v. Hardacher	DEFDEPSUM
Cucurri v. Gardner A/K/A	SIMONDEPSUM
Charlton Co. v. Barron	REIMERDEPSUM
Darrin v. State Farm Insurance	PTFDEPSUM
Donovan v. O'Hara Brokerage	DENNYDEPSUM
Easton, Inc. v. Doherty Corp.	HILLDEPSUM
Fenton v. Rose	PTFDEPSUM
Fitz v. Zelda	REPDEPSUM
Garrett v. Daily	MASDEPSUM
Grace v. Ernest	DEFDEPSUM
Halloway Tectronics v. Albert	EXPERTDEPSUM
Ionia Development Corp. v. Baker	DEFDEPSUM
Kable v. Allstate Insurance	RODHAMDEPSUM
Lake v. Christopher	MAITLINDEPSUM
Miller v. O'Neill	PTFDEPSUM
Miller v. O'Neill	DEFDEPSUM
Page v. Bottle Realty Co.	ELLIOTTDEPSUM
Queen Corp. v. Bailey Printing	PTFDEPSUM
Roehr v. Allison Partners	TINKERDEPSUM
Stuart v. Teterond	ARGYLDEPSUM
Temple v. Atchison	PTFDEPSUM
Virdon v. Osteen	HERTERDEPSUM

She sighed.

She pulled up the first file:

ARLISS VERSUS HARDACHER
Summary of the Deposition of Steven Arliss

PAGE	LINE	TESTIMONY
1–6	—	Background: 36; BA (Econ) UMd (1980); no armed forces exp.; Wk. Hist.: 1980–1983, Baltimore Graphics (sales); 1983–1989, Wilson Sporting Goods (sales); 1989–Present, Annapolis Brokers (sales); left each position of own volition, seeking "greater challenge" and "better opportunity."

Marjorie stopped reading. She asked Word Search to find "Highways to Indians." It came up with nothing.

She sighed again. This was shaping up as a long afternoon.

A gentle rain was falling by the time Michaelson reached the modest house of ocher-colored brick in McLean, Virginia, where Artemus lived. He found the retired general kneeling at the near border of a flower bed that seemed to occupy a third of the backyard. Squishing through the drizzle-beaded grass, Michaelson introduced himself, shook hands, then pointed at an empty steel bucket a couple of yards away.

"May I?" he asked.

"Be my guest."

Sissy Artemus, who had let Michaelson into the house and directed him to the backyard, had warned him that her husband might grant an audience but certainly would not allow his gardening to be interrupted. Michaelson turned the bucket upside down and sat on its bottom, grimacing only slightly as accumulated damp seeped through the seat of his pants.

What would most people think a warrior looked like? Michaelson wondered, reflecting on several he had known. Not, surely, like Artemus, with his avuncular face, his thinning red hair plastered across his brown-blotched scalp, his slightly thickened middle bulging a bit over the black leather belt at his waist. Had Artemus lost that special cold fire sometime in the late seventies or early eighties, felt it flicker out late some sleepless night while he thought about brave men and frightened boys under his command who'd been sacrificed a few years before to electoral calculations?

Michaelson thought he could tell if he could see the man's eyes. But he couldn't do that right now.

"Do you know why I've come?" he asked.

"Define 'know,'" Artemus said as he worked his fingers lovingly through rich loam. "Sorry. Inside joke. You've come because you want to learn something."

"Actually, I'm here because I want to understand something I've already learned," Michaelson said. "I know Jeffrey Quentin offered you a return to active duty, a shot at a plum assignment, and *de facto* rehabilitation of your career. I know you turned him down. But I want to understand why."

"Now, how do you figure you know all that?" Artemus asked the question in a gently joshing tone, without taking his eyes off the viscous soil he was kneading.

"The first part is simply the standard Quentin bribe adapted to your situation. I know he offered that to you because he offered the functional equivalent to me, and you have a lot more to give him in exchange than I do. I know you turned him down because he hasn't delivered and he's the type who knows better than to breach illegitimate contracts."

"Are you sure you're as smart as you think you are?" Artemus asked in the same voice as before.

"Not entirely. But the important thing in Washington is to be smarter than other people think you are. I've managed that much for over forty years now."

"Then why do you need anything Quentin could give you?"

"I don't. I *want* something he could give me, but that's not the same thing."

Artemus sat back on his heels and laboriously scooted his knees sideways until he was giving Michaelson about a three-quarter profile. He gazed with deeply hooded eyes at the older man.

"Don't bullshit me," he said jovially. "I know about you. I remembered your name the minute Sissy told me you'd called. You got yourself talked about plenty when I was working at the White House."

"I'm flattered," Michaelson said. "When you were at the White House I was either rather old for an area director or rather young for a retired foreign service officer."

"You retired early from the State Department, but you weren't pushed out. You decided on your own to leave because you wanted to set yourself up for national security adviser or CIA director. Everyone including the tour guides knew that."

"I'm an ambitious man," Michaelson conceded mildly. "But a large part of the jobs I want amounts to drawing lines.

A national security adviser who's willing to do anything the president wants him to is worse than dangerous—he's useless. There are things I won't do to get those jobs, because there are things I'd have to refuse to do if I got them."

"That's easy to say from the sidelines."

"I've had plenty of practice. I've been on the sidelines a long time now."

"If I were you, I'd take up gardening," Artemus said.

He grinned bitterly as he said this. With the grin his eyes opened wide, and Michaelson saw the fire: banked, perhaps, but not gone. He realized that it must be killing Artemus to kneel here tending roses instead of planning troop movements or plotting procurement strategy.

"I'm not going to waste your time," Michaelson said. "You had a choice when Quentin approached you. You made it and in my judgment you made it correctly. You refused to cross the line. What matters right now, though, is *why* you made the choice you did. You're the only one who can answer that question for me. If you're willing to answer it, I'm eager to hear what you have to say. If you're not willing to answer it, I'll go nurse my frustration someplace a little bit drier."

"Why does it matter?" Artemus asked.

"A woman named Sharon Bedford died young about ten days ago. She shouldn't have. The answer to my question has something to do with her death and therefore with her life. That's why it matters."

Michaelson felt that he'd passed some kind of a test. Sighing briefly, Artemus gathered up a trowel and a mini-rake.

"I guess I did it because I wanted to face a choice like that and get it right while there was still time," he said. "Let's go inside."

★

Whatever paralegals get paid, Marjorie thought fiercely, it's not enough. No amount would be adequate compensation for wading through these dreary, tedious, repetitious exercises in finger-pointing, blame-shifting, evasion, and self-justification —much less for finding the few nuggets of substantive information buried in there and bringing them out. She had stolen more than two precious hours from the limitless demands of Cavalier Books, devoted them to slogging doggedly through deposition summaries prepared by Sharon Bedford, and come up with nothing.

She now knew that the phrase "Highways to Indians" wasn't nestled conveniently within any of the summaries, at least in any obvious way. She knew that the six summaries she had read from beginning to end overflowed with mind-numbing detail about dozens of things that shouldn't have led to the murder of Sharon Bedford or anyone else, except perhaps a couple of lawyers. And she knew that she had to find a better way to do this.

The disk listed the deposition summaries in alphabetical order, by case name. Hoping with a combination of desperation and giddiness that putting them in chronological order might suggest something more promising than she'd come up with so far, she rummaged through piles on her desk until she found the neatly typed invoices Bedford had sent to Hayes & Barthelt for her work. The invoices themselves were dated and each summary charged for on an invoice also bore a date, so it was easy for Marjorie to list the summaries from earliest to latest on a legal pad.

Having done so, she contemplated her handiwork. Nothing. Calling the disk directory back to her computer screen, she compared her handwritten, chronological list with the electronic, alphabetical list. Nothing.

Except that the handwritten list was shorter. Nuts. She must have missed one. Which? A quick check disclosed *Cucurri v. Gardner a/k/a* as the summary missing from the handwritten list.

She thumbed back through the invoices. *Cucurri v. Gardner a/k/a* wasn't there. Bedford apparently hadn't charged Hayes & Barthelt for summarizing a deposition in that case.

Marjorie retrieved the Cucurri summary and clicked down to the end. END OF DEPOSITION. All caps. So Bedford had finished the summary. But she apparently hadn't billed for it. Why? Whatever the reason might be, the only place Marjorie could think of to look for it was in the summary itself. So that's what she began doing.

"Did you know it's possible to have a totally secret court-martial in this country?" Artemus was asking Michaelson about the time Marjorie began reading the Cucurri summary. "I mean absolute star chamber. Locked and guarded courtroom. Sealed evidence. No public notice of charges or outcome. And if anyone goes looking for it later on—brother, it just didn't happen."

"No," Michaelson said. "I didn't know that, as a matter of fact."

They were sitting across a simple wooden table in the Artemus kitchen, mugs of steaming coffee before them.

"It's a fact. That's what they threatened me with. They were serious, too."

"Well, it's nice to have an intuition confirmed now and then," Michaelson said. "They didn't threaten you with something like that over shoving your way to the head of the line outside an operating room.''

"You said your question mattered because a woman died who didn't have to die,'' Artemus said after a long sip of scalding coffee. "That's the way I felt about my daughter. I had a lever. If I didn't use it, she was going to die and she didn't have to die. It was just as simple as that.''

"It's the lever I'm really interested in.''

"Right.''

"But you're not going to tell me what it was.''

"Can't.''

"After all,'' Michaelson said, "being court-martialed isn't the kind of thing any prudent soldier would risk twice.''

Artemus smiled without showing his teeth, amused rather than provoked by the artless gibe.

"You probably aren't going to believe it, not that I care particularly, but that's not it. Fact is, it wasn't the court-martial threat that made me cave in and retire.''

"What was it, then?'' Michaelson asked.

"I just looked at what I'd done, and looked back at the way it had all happened, and I knew I'd flat gotten it wrong. I don't mean when I helped my daughter, I mean from the beginning. I step into the White House, get one look at the inside of the Oval Office, and overnight every instinct I had turned to crap. First time it had ever happened. Once I realized that, I had less confidence in myself than I'd had when I was a plebe at the Point.''

"You astound me,'' Michaelson confessed. "If someone had asked me to dream up twenty possible explanations for what happened to you, that one wouldn't have been on the list.''

"It was just so different to be in the middle of it while it was happening. I mean, there on the scene, at the time, everything seemed to make perfectly good sense."

" 'While it was happening,' " Michaelson repeated pensively.

"You know what I mean. People today tend to feel warm and fuzzy when they think back on President Reagan's foreign policy, 'cause by the time he left office, the Berlin Wall was about to come down, the Soviet Union was about to bust apart, we'd just about won the Cold War, and you figure somewhere along in there someone must've done something right. But I'll tell you what, when it was going on and no one knew for sure how any of that was going to come out, the whole thing looked just a tad dicier."

Michaelson waited, raising his eyebrows encouragingly, giving Artemus a chance to say the obvious, to cite the two irrefutable concrete examples of the nerveracking diciness he'd just asserted: the Iran/Contra mess; and the nearly disastrous summit in Reykjavik, where President Reagan had come within a stunning, naive inch of giving away the nuclear advantage of the United States without getting anything in return.

Artemus didn't cite them. Returning to the enigmatic half-smile he'd used earlier, he simply stopped talking.

Michaelson sagged a bit in his chair. The flicker of hopeful expectation that had flared briefly inside him when Artemus began to open up guttered.

"There is one potentially useful thing you can tell me," Michaelson said then. "One thing that won't further compound the error you feel you made, and could conceivably mitigate it."

"What's that?" Artemus asked skeptically.

"Whom did you co-opt to get the special treatment you wanted for your daughter?"

Artemus considered the question for a moment before he showed his teeth in a malicious grin.

"Dr. Marc," he said. "Jerry Marciniak, p-h-*fucking*-d. You get a chance, you just mitigate the *hell* out of him, far as I'm concerned."

★

". . . a totally fresh biography of Gladstone," the eager sales rep from HarperCollins who'd come in when Marjorie was two-thirds of the way through the deposition summary in *Cucurri v. Gardner a/k/a* said. "Emphasizes his human side, if you get my drift."

"I don't think most of my customers are terribly interested in S&M," Marjorie said. "You might try Brentano's on that one."

"No, really," the rep said. "Kirkus said this biography was 'two steps above *God Is an Englishman.*' "

"I remember reading that," Marjorie said. "I believe that comment was intended to be disparaging."

"My whole point," the rep said delightedly, spreading his arms over the attaché case perched on his knees. "A heaping tablespoon of sugar to help the history go down. Not history for people who already know history, history for people who love to read. Connecticut Avenue demographics on the nose."

Grinning, Marjorie relaxed, her sales resistance overcome by the irrefutable argument.

"Send me two copies," she said. "I'll sell the first one to a retiring lobbyist and rely on word of mouth to sell the second."

"You won't be sorry," the rep promised as he opened his attaché case and made quick notations in his order book. "Hey, I have a great bookstore joke for you."

"I hope it's a quick one," Marjorie said. "I've spent all afternoon on a problem that has nothing to do with keeping this store profitable, and I haven't gotten anywhere with it."

The rep snapped his case shut and stood up.

"Very quick. Salesman's racing through an airport. Realizes he forgot to bring anything to read on the flight. Passes a bookstore and notices a book on its remainders table, right inside the front door: *Secrets to Sex*. Sign underneath says 'For Sale to Adults Only.' Sounds like it might not be too bad. Hears his flight being called. Grabs the book, throws his money at the clerk, hustles to the gate, and gets on board. Settles back for some salacious delight, opens the book, and discovers that he's bought volume nineteen of *Graham's Encyclopedic Manual of Grammar, Diction and Usage*."

The square-faced man's wire-rimmed glasses twinkled as he waited through two seconds of anxious silence. All at once Marjorie's face was blank, her eyes seemingly fixed on a horizon somewhere well beyond the storeroom at Cavalier Books.

"Come on," he pleaded. "It wasn't *that* bad."

To his considerable alarm Marjorie suddenly leaped from her chair.

"It is a perfectly marvelous joke, the best joke I've heard in Washington since the last time Congress tried to define middle class," she assured him in a delighted voice. Seizing his shoulders, she spun him effortlessly toward the door. "Now scoot. I have to think."

As soon as she'd hustled the slightly bewildered man out the door, Marjorie hurried, laughing, back to her desk.

I've been had, she thought to herself between fits of giggles. We've all been had. There wasn't any road map in the Cucurri deposition summary. The entire thing was window dressing. Classic red herring. Bedford had simply put this imaginary name on a duplicate summary of another deposition. Her own little private joke. Like the *Illegitimi Non Carborundum* plate she'd given Davidson.

Marjorie's giggles turned into a full-throated laugh. She could see Bedford, the NSC staff veteran, chortling to herself as she thought of someone stealing her computer files, laboring feverishly over them, and then racing furiously down the false trail Bedford had deliberately created.

Because that's what the case name was. A confection that an NSC computer would have identified in thirty minutes as a tantalizing lead, and which would then have sent hordes of researchers hustling up a blind alley. As *Illegitimi Non Carborundum* and the rest of the scene in Davidson's tiny office flashed through her mind once again, Marjorie was certain of it.

"Carrie?" she called, scurrying onto the sales floor.

"Yes?" Carrie answered patiently as she simultaneously propped a telephone receiver between her ear and shoulder and rang up a sale.

"Where's our last copy of Lewis and Short?"

"Reference section, foreign language gondola, bottom shelf, toward the far end."

Marjorie found *A Latin Dictionary* by Charlton T. Lewis and Charles Short exactly where Carrie said it was. She had the bulky tome open in her hands and was eagerly reading from it even before she'd made it back to the stockroom.

Five minutes later she was back on the sales floor, hurrying toward the front door.

"I'll try to be back by five-thirty," she told Carrie breathlessly on her way out.

Carrie took advantage of the first respite from the late-afternoon trickle of customers to find the legal pad on Marjorie's desk and satisfy her curiosity about the sudden exit. The respite lasted about ninety seconds. This proved ample.

Like all respectable practitioners of the bookseller's craft, Carrie knew that Erle Stanley Gardner, creator of Perry Mason, also wrote mysteries under the pen name A. A. Fair. And so she had no difficulty at all in understanding Marjorie's telegraphic notes:

> *Currere* = To run
> *Curo* = I run
> *Cucurri* = I ran
> v. = *versus* = *contra*
> Gardner a/k/a = A. A. Fair
> *Cucurri v. Gardner a/k/a* = I ran contra A. A. Fair
> = Iran/Contra Affair.

chapter

14

★

Michaelson reminded himself that paranoia is generally unbecoming, particularly in someone old enough to know better.
Him, for example. Still, he couldn't shake the feeling.

He had gotten to Cavalier Books just after four-thirty, to be
met with Carrie's announcement that Marjorie had departed
in considerable haste, half an hour or so before. She hadn't
actually announced her destination, but Carrie and Marjorie
had talked about Sharon Bedford before today. Putting two
and two together, Carrie had concluded that Marjorie was
headed back to Hayes & Barthelt, the main law firm for which
Sharon Bedford had freelanced. She'd given every indication
of thinking she was on to something, and the notes she'd left
on her desk confirmed that inference.

It was at this point that Michaelson had sensed paranoia's
first seductive advances. What were the chances that Pilkington or Quentin had had him followed? Small but nontrivial, in
foreign service jargon. He'd seen no sign of anything like that,
but of course if the people who were doing it were good
enough, he wouldn't have. If he was being followed, what
were the chances that he'd led the tail to Cavalier Books? A

hundred percent. So was there a genuine risk that Marjorie was being followed as well? Should he rush after her, like Don Quixote in an aging Omni?

Of course not, he realized as he relaxed a bit. If he wasn't being followed, he'd feel silly; and if he was, he'd only increase whatever risk Marjorie faced by joining her.

He settled for calling the law firm and verifying that Marjorie had indeed arrived and was now closeted with the head paralegal, Mr. Davidson. Did he wish to ring Mr. Davidson's office?

He did not. He wished the receptionist to ask Marjorie to call him before leaving. The receptionist promised that she would.

"If you ask me how I came up with this question," Marjorie was telling Davidson, "I'll be too embarrassed to tell you. So please just humor me."

"Trust me," Davidson said. "I've been dealing with lawyers for twenty-seven years."

"Okay. Are there such things as legal encyclopedias—attorneys' equivalents of *Britannica* or *Americana*?"

"Sure. The two most popular are *American Jurisprudence Second* and *Corpus Juris Secundum*—AmJur and CJS to the initiated."

"Do either of those have a volume titled 'Highways to Indians'?"

"You're right," Davidson said, "that question is off the wall. One way to find out."

Thumbing through compact discs in a plastic box beside his computer, he chose one and popped it into the machine. After forty-five seconds he took it out and turned back toward Marjorie.

"The answers in order are no and no," he said.

Marjorie slumped a bit.

"I was hoping for different answers," she confessed.

"That's often the case with people who ask me questions," Davidson said. "Like that guy who interrupted us yesterday. I'm sure he wanted a bright-line rule for choice of law, and I had to give him a five-factor balancing test."

"And you didn't take long to do it," Marjorie said, brightening a bit. "You got a legal research assignment, and the first thing you did was pull out a comprehensive list of legal topics so that you could research the question on your computer."

"Right."

"The list put the topics in alphabetical order, didn't it?"

"Yep."

"May I see it?"

"Sure," Davidson said. "In the off-the-wall competition, by the way, you've just rung the bell again."

After rummaging a bit, Davidson handed over the page. Her fingers shaking just a bit from suppressed excitement as she turned it over, Marjorie scanned down the first closely printed column on the reverse side. For her purposes, the column began provocatively:

GUARANTY
GUARDIAN AND WARD
HABEAS CORPUS
HAWKERS AND PEDDLERS
HEALTH AND ENVIRONMENT
HIGHWAYS

HOLIDAYS
HOMESTEAD
HOMICIDE
HOSPITALS
HUSBAND AND WIFE
ILLEGITIMATE CHILDREN
IMPLIED AND CONSTRUCTIVE CONTRACTS
IMPROVEMENTS
INCEST
INDEMNITY
INDIANS

"I remember you saying that, in the old days, people used to look for the law in books instead of computer databases," she said.

"And some still do," Davidson said, nodding.

"If you wanted to do the assignment you did yesterday by looking in a book, where would you look?"

"I'd start with the first half of the tenth series of the West Publishing Company's *Decennial Digest*, covering the period 1986 to 1991. It's basically sixty volumes of one-paragraph case notes, organized according to the topics on that list."

"Can you show me?" Marjorie asked.

"Nothing to it."

Crushing his cigarette and heaving himself from his chair, Davidson led Marjorie down a hall and up a small, winding staircase to the firm's law library. He walked her to a massive set of shelves near an array of carrels and gestured grandly toward three-score massive tomes. They all said *Tenth Decennial Digest*. A subtitle added "Part 1 1986 to 1991."

As Davidson's description had indicated, the volumes were

divided by topic ranges, like an encyclopedia set. Volume 22 was "Game to Homicide." Volume 23 was "Homicide to Infants." "Highways to Indians" didn't appear.

Marjorie felt the acid bite of bitter disappointment, but she refused to accept the verdict. Conclusions reasoned to by implacable logic could be wrong, she felt; intuitive certainties couldn't be. At least *her* intuitive certainties.

"If there's a *Tenth Decennial Digest*, there must be a *Ninth*," she said.

"In storage," Davidson said. He pointed at closed cupboards just below ceiling level. "At sixty volumes a crack and three thousand pages a volume, those things eat up space, and lawyers won't cite cases more than ten years old if they don't have to. That's one of the reasons West has them on-line now."

"Might I take a look?"

"I don't see why not. No crazier than anything else we've done in the last fifteen minutes."

Davidson found a wheeled step stool and pulled it several shelf widths down the aisle. He offered Marjorie his hand. Kicking off her low heels, she stepped onto the small and, it seemed to her, none-too-steady platform. Trying to blot the vivid image of a broken ankle from her mind, she gritted her teeth and pried the cupboard door open.

The volumes were stacked on their sides. She had to turn her head slightly sideways and read laboriously up the third stack she could see. Volume 20: "Embezzlement to Executors and Administrators." Volume 21: "Exemptions to Federal Civil Procedure." Volume 22: "Federal Civil Procedure to Federal Courts." Volume 23: "Fences to Health and Environment." And then, on the spine of the fifth volume in the third stack, she found the precious words she was looking for:

NINTH DECENNIAL DIGEST
Part 2
1981 to 1986
HIGHWAYS TO INDIANS

Brownish-red binding dust erupted from the cupboard and mustily tickled her nose as she worked that tome out from between the books above and below it. It was about the length and width of a standard volume of the *Oxford English Dictionary.* Cradling it in the crook of her left arm, she let Davidson help her down from the step stool. She lugged the massive book over to the nearest carrel and laid it delicately on the desk.

"You may want to go over and get me volume twenty-four of the tenth digest while I'm glancing through here," she said to Davidson.

"Why? Do you want to compare that one with this one?"

"No," Marjorie said, looking directly at him. "But it's quite likely that anything I find in here will have gotten Sharon Bedford killed, and it occurs to me that you might not want to know about it."

"Suppose it implicates the firm in some way," Davidson said.

"Then it probably wouldn't be hidden in this library. But I'll promise you that if it does reflect on the firm, you'll get a heads-up before I show it to anyone else."

"Fair enough," Davidson said. "I'll appreciate the signal. Most important, though, you make sure whoever killed Sharon gets nailed, and I'll be happy." He sidled away.

After a few seconds of frustrated riffling, Marjorie found what she was looking for taped to the volume's inside back cover. It was a plain white business envelope, stamped but not postmarked, and addressed to Sharon Bedford.

The hiding place struck her as perfect. The book would probably never be used. Even if "Highways to Indians" was pulled down once in a blue moon, someone could read case digests in it for two hours without spotting the envelope. And if by some wild chance someone did come across it, they'd almost certainly just drop it in the mail to Bedford or at least contact her before they opened it. Bedford would have been justly confident that she could hide the envelope in this book as long as she needed to, and retrieve it whenever she wanted it.

Marjorie tucked the envelope in her purse.

"All clear?" Davidson asked from between two shelves a second or so later.

"Yes," Marjorie said, finding to her astonishment that she was short of breath.

When she reached the reception area a few minutes later, her belly did a nauseating little flip. She noticed two men standing in the elevator lobby just beyond the massive glass doors that marked the main entrance to the firm. She told herself firmly that there was nothing intrinsically sinister about two men waiting for an elevator outside a law firm around quitting time. Her belly flipped again.

The men were wearing dark suits, white shirts, and dark ties. As Marjorie focused her full powers of concentration on the pair, she saw that they had beady, reptilian eyes, predatory curves to the thin, bloodless lips that defined their mouths, empty faces devoid of human warmth, and generally chilling demeanors.

It was then that the receptionist favored her with Michaelson's message. Marjorie called the bookstore from a phone on a table behind the receptionist's desk and quickly reached Michaelson.

"I hope I don't sound too alarmist," Michaelson said apologetically after he'd explained his concerns. "But I did think it possible that you'd have unwanted company by now."

"You don't sound at all alarmist to me," Marjorie said. "In fact, there are two rather sinister-looking males loitering in the elevator lobby."

"There's no need to make fun of my caution, however excessive it appears," Michaelson said.

"On the contrary, there is immense need to make fun of it, but as it happens, I'm speaking quite literally."

"Why don't you check with the receptionist and see if she recognizes them?" Michaelson suggested.

"Yes, I think so," Marjorie said. Taking the phone from her ear and turning toward the receptionist's back, she stage-whispered, "Excuse me, do you know who those two gentlemen standing out by the elevators are?"

"Those aren't any gentlemen," the receptionist said scornfully over her shoulder. "They're personal-injury plaintiffs' lawyers down here from New York for depositions that just finished up."

Marjorie put the phone back to her ear.

"You can relax," she told Michaelson. "Our fears were perfectly plausible but ultimately unfounded."

chapter

15

★

Somehow," Marjorie said, "I thought that when I finally stumbled across a written document of immense importance, it would be a little less prosaic. You know, a palimpsest with an indictment of cruelty to bulls that was omitted by a printer's error from the published version of *The Sun Also Rises*. Something along those lines."

"This will do, believe me," Michaelson said in a deeply preoccupied voice as he gestured briefly with the single page he held.

They were sitting in his Georgetown apartment, where the smell of mediocre pepperoni and decent Cabernet still lingered. It was just after seven o'clock.

The paper Michaelson held was high-quality, eighty-pound, watermarked bond. DINAR, stamped in oversized red letters, was centered at the top. In the upper left-hand corner, a string of numerals sandwiched around a single letter appeared: 87-14159195A003. Each character in the sequence was formed by a series of pin-sized holes machine-cut into the page.

A pebbled, red-and-blue border framed the array. After

the last numeral, the words RAISED PRINTING DO NOT PHOTO-
COPY appeared in small black typeface against the same
pebbled, red-and-blue background. A thumb-rub over the
words confirmed that they were embossed and not merely
printed.

It took Michaelson less than thirty seconds to read and
absorb the document's text:

TO: GEN WP ARTEMUS MIL LIAISON OP WASH DC
      GEN LR MECKSTROTH HQ/NATO BRUX
      KR MCCRAFT NSC STAFF LIAISON WASH DC

GREETINGS

EFFECTIVE THIS DATE THROUGH NOON EST 1/20/89 THE
FOLLOWING CATEGORIES ORDERS REQUIRE SAY AGAIN RE-
QUIRE APPROVAL STAT CHR NSC PRIOR SAY AGAIN PRIOR
EXECUTION:

1. INITIATION CATEGORY 1 FORCES
2. ALTERATION RULES OF ENGAGEMENT US/FRIENDLY
    FORCES ETO
3. HOSTILE INITIATION SEA/LAND/AIR FORCES PRINCIPAL
    AREAS POTENTIAL ENGAGEMENT
EXCEPTIONS: NONE
COUNTERMAND: WCS ONLY.

The document was dated November 2, 1987. It bore a
signature—or a purported signature—that Michaelson had
seen many times.

"What does 'DINAR' mean?" Marjorie asked.

"It's a security classification," Michaelson said distractedly.

"Like 'Top Secret'?"

"Like that, but considerably more restrictive. Literally thousands of people have top-secret security clearances. If a document is classified 'Top Secret/Sensitive/Eyes Only for the President,' about two hundred people would be cleared to see it. A document stamped 'DINAR' can legally be shown to only thirty-one human beings on earth. Technically, you and I have probably just committed espionage."

" 'OP' is Office of the President, presumably, since that's where Artemus was at the time this was prepared," Marjorie said. " 'Rules of engagement' are when, how, and under what circumstances you can fight. Even I know that. And it doesn't take a genius to figure out that two and three are talking about NATO and the Fifth and Seventh Fleets."

"Not to mention the marines on Diego Garcia and two combat-ready divisions in South Korea."

"What are category one forces?"

"Nuclear weapons."

"Which ones?" Marjorie asked.

"All of them. ICBMs, Strategic Air Command, submarine-launched ballistic missiles, cruise missiles surface to surface or air to surface, and anything else that those clever engineers out in California cooked up before they lost their jobs."

"And what does 'WCS' mean?"

"Literally it stands for 'written, cut, and signed.' In other words, this order could only be countermanded by an order that was in writing, was signed by an officer or official with adequate authority, and had an authenticating confirmation number cut into it—just as this one did. More colloquially, because of the inflexibility that a designation like that implies, officers sometimes joke that 'WCS' stands for 'worst case scenario.' "

"I shouldn't ask because it only encourages you," Marjorie said, "but I really do want to know. What does the 'STAT C-H-R N-S-C' business refer to?"

"The statutory chairman of the national security council," Michaelson said. "Or in plain English, the vice president of the United States."

"I find myself a little uncomfortable with the implications of this."

"If it weren't for the pose of blasé sophistication that I feel called upon to affect, I'd find myself appalled beyond imagination by its implications," Michaelson said.

"Well," Marjorie allowed after she'd drained her glass of wine, "in the genteel society in which I was raised, 'appalled beyond imagination' is pretty much what 'a little uncomfortable' means."

"If this document is authentic," Michaelson said, "this country underwent the first coup d'état in its history on November 2, 1987. The president of the United States was effectively relieved of his constitutional authority as commander-in-chief of the armed forces. Counting the addressees, there are seven—no, eight people who absolutely had to be in on it. At least one of those people is quite likely to be on the presidential ticket of a major party within three months. This piece of paper is the plainest documentary proof of treason since—since I don't know when."

"Since South Carolina's ordinance of secession in 1860, presumably," Marjorie said as her rich Southern accent deepened. Pausing thoughtfully, she refilled her wineglass and took another long sip. "Is it actually possible?" she asked then.

"Thinking back on things, it seems not only possible but stunningly plausible," Michaelson said. "It certainly fits in with Artemus's morose ruminations this afternoon. When Iran/Contra was at its absolute worst inside the Beltway, when it seemed that it had completely paralyzed the administration, I remember seeing a flurry of obviously planted stories in the *Post* and the *Times* suggesting that unnamed aides thought that President Reagan was under undue mental strain."

"As if they were trying to set things up to ease him out of office early under the Twenty-fifth Amendment—claim that he was mentally disabled and replace him?"

"That's what I thought at the time. Then the effort suddenly disappeared without a trace, and I assumed that it was just one of those nice tries that didn't quite get off the ground."

"Whereas it may simply have become unnecessary," Marjorie said.

"Yes. After this order circulated, any removal effort that was actually authorized by the Constitution would have been exquisitely superfluous."

"What now?" Marjorie asked.

"They say that it pays to advertise," Michaelson said. "I think our next move is to do something fairly conspicuous."

"Wait a minute. Are you going to tell Gallagher about this?"

"Yes."

"I expect he's going to be rather conspicuous around Washington himself about two hours after you do," Marjorie said.

"I expect the same thing."

"Won't we be putting him in danger by inviting attention to ourselves, then?"

"You're right." Pausing, Michaelson finished his wine and gazed reflectively at the goblet. "I suppose we'd better think up some non-Washington task to keep him busy for a day or two."

"Good luck," Marjorie said.

She rose to refill her glass, thought better of it, and sat back down. In what anyone but Michaelson might have taken as some agitation, she looked around the familiar room as if she'd never seen it before. Finally, resting her forearms on her crossed legs, she leaned forward.

"Was the vice president one of the eight people who had to be in the middle of it?" she asked.

"No."

"Do you think he knew?"

"Define 'know,' " Michaelson replied.

chapter

16

★

The dull-finish metal box nestled inside the wooden cabinet above the gas stove in Michaelson's kitchenette as if it had been die-cut and laser-trimmed to the cabinet's dimensions. Someone poking his nose into the cabinet would see what looked like the outside of a ventilating shaft.

"This is the key," Gallagher said, holding up a notched cylinder an eighth of an inch in diameter and two inches long.

He stuck the cylinder into what looked like a rivet head in the lower right-hand corner of the box's face. A gentle click sounded when he turned the cylinder. The front of the box popped open from the bottom, revealing that it wasn't wafer-thin tinplate but half an inch of carbonized steel.

Michaelson and Marjorie watched the performance with polite interest. It was just after three in the afternoon, not quite twenty-four hours after Marjorie's discovery of the November 2, 1987, order hidden by Sharon Bedford. Michaelson had called Gallagher the evening before, suggesting an off-hand hope that he might be able to come up to Washington over the weekend. Gallagher had been on a flight first thing the following morning and, once he understood the problem, had gotten a Deluxe Secure Hideaway LokBox delivered first thing that afternoon.

"We have almost a thousand of these installed around the country, with an absolute guarantee against forcible entry or removal. We've only gotten one claim, and that turned out to be an insurance fraud setup."

"Very impressive," Michaelson said. He took a sealed white envelope from his inside coat pocket, slipped it into the lockbox, and snapped the cover shut. He returned a collection of cellophane-wrapped napkins and paper-towel rolls to the cabinet and swung its door shut. Then he led Gallagher and Marjorie out of the tiny kitchen area and into a somewhat larger living room.

"Let's review what we have so far," he said. "Three people with an established or presumptive interest in the November order are known to have visited Sharon Bedford in her hotel room the morning she died: Jerry Marciniak, Jeffrey Quentin, and Scott Pilkington."

"What's Marciniak's presumptive interest?" Marjorie asked as the three seated themselves.

"Marciniak rose from a humdrum civil service slot in the health-care bureaucracy to a major policy-making position," Michaelson said. "He did so with unbecoming speed. A suggestively short time before that ascent began, according to Artemus, Artemus used Marciniak to get his daughter priority for critical medical treatment. Artemus did that by using the order—the 'lever,' as he put it. The order would give him leverage with Marciniak only if Marciniak thought he could use his knowledge of the order to his own advantage later on. The sharp hostility to Marciniak that Artemus expressed suggests that Marciniak did exactly that, and did it almost immediately, thereby exposing what Artemus had done."

"Used it to boost his own meteoric rise, you mean," Marjorie said.

"Yes."

"I'm convinced," Marjorie said. "Sorry about sidetracking your summary. You had placed three suspects in Sharon Bedford's room the morning she was killed."

"Except that we're going to have to come up with some creative thinking to turn either Quentin or Marciniak into a legitimate suspect," Michaelson said.

"I'm glad I'm not the only one worried about that," Gallagher said. "The killer poisoned Sharon by injecting bufotenine into a mint she ate. The maid didn't leave the mint in her room until just before Sharon left the café where she was eating breakfast, and by that time both Marciniak and Quentin had long since come and gone."

"What a depressing display of left-brained, logic-bound, linear Western thinking," Marjorie said.

"But hard to argue with," Michaelson commented.

"That's what's so depressing about it," Marjorie said.

"Well, all that means is that we have one more question to answer before we have the solution," Michaelson said. "There's an objection nearly as substantial to Pilkington as the killer. If he tampered with the mint, he had to do so while Ms. Bedford was in the room. He might have been able to accomplish that by distracting her and going through some sleight of hand. But he couldn't have counted on that when he was planning the murder."

"The solution doesn't leap out at me," Marjorie said. "But at least we can be reasonably sure Pilkington and Quentin knew Bedford had a duplicate original of the order. They knew about the order, and they had to realize that that was what she was hinting about in her job hustle."

"Marciniak knew about the order, too, and she was also hustling him for a job," Michaelson pointed out.

"Right," Marjorie said. "But we have no reason to believe she was using the order to do it. Marciniak denied that she was shopping anything to him. We don't have any hard evidence that he was lying. He might have heard she was claiming at the conference to have something juicy up her sleeve, but the murder had to have been planned before the conference. No one just happened to waltz down there with bufotenine in his pocket. I think that if we're going to pin her murder on Marciniak, we're going to have to show that he had some way of knowing exactly what Sharon had, and some reason to want to keep her from using it."

"And as if all of those problems weren't daunting enough," Michaelson said, "Marciniak, Quentin, and Pilkington are only the people that someone spotted going into Ms. Bedford's room. We can't be certain that they're the only possible suspects."

"Can you think of any others?" Gallagher asked.

Before answering, Michaelson rose lightly from his chair and crossed to a drink caddy near the window.

"I have the standard selections," he said as he opened a bottle of Johnny Walker Black Label scotch and poured two fingers into a crystal tumbler that he took from the caddy's bottom shelf. "Can I get anything for anyone else?"

"G&T, naturally." Gallagher shrugged.

"Scotch," Marjorie said.

Michaelson deliberately prepared and distributed the requested drinks, sank back into his chair, took one sip from his own glass, then smiled benignly at the other two for a moment before speaking.

"There is at least one other suspect," he said. "And I think the next thing we have to decide is whether to focus on him or cross him off the list."

"Who's that?" Marjorie asked.

"Alex Moodie. He was there, he was intensely interested in retrieving his wife's career, and when I talked to the two of them, Deborah told me a couple of deliberate lies. Or to be fair, made a couple of key statements that were incompletely truthful. She did so for what I'd regard as fairly noble reasons, but she still didn't come across with all the facts."

"You going to expand on that for us?" Gallagher asked after putting a substantial dent in his gin and tonic.

"When her initial push on the Artemus matter went no-where," Michaelson said, "Deborah did what any savvy and experienced bureaucrat would do. She stopped pushing. Then, years later, she resumed the crusade. She told me that that happened out of sheer frustration. That wasn't the whole truth."

"What is?" Marjorie asked.

"I don't know. But I think finding out should become a priority at the Washington end of our little adventure."

" 'Washington end'?" Gallagher asked. "What other end is there?"

"There's a loose thread in Wilmot, Ohio, that we've been ignoring," Michaelson said.

"The phony, obscene birthday card that was found in Sharon's room, you mean," Gallagher said.

"Exactly. It connects to Quentin, obviously, but what exactly is the connection? The card as a blackmail instrument doesn't work very well. Is there something more substantial? Specifically, is there some link between Ms. Bedford and one of the victims of the campaign ploy involving that card that Quentin orchestrated?"

"Any ideas about how to answer that question?" Gallagher asked.

"One," Michaelson said. "It involves you."

He explained what he had in mind.

"That seems a little bit, ah, off-center," Gallagher said.

"Agreed," Michaelson said. "If a straight-ahead attack could expose the murderer, the Charleston police would presumably have him in custody by now."

"I'm game," Gallagher sighed.

"Happy hunting," Michaelson said.

★

When he pulled up across the street from the tidy, working-class duplex in Wilmot, Ohio, Gallagher got a gut-wrench worse than the one that preceded the first sales call he'd ever made. It wasn't quite paralyzing, but it was bad enough to make him forget for a moment the brain-numbing fatigue that pulsed through his body after the six hours of cabs, planes, shuttle buses, and rental cars that separated him right now from Washington.

He'd been doubtful from the beginning about even finding the woman. He was a salesman, not an analyst. He hadn't seen the inside of a library since college. He couldn't believe that he could just walk up to the ready reference desk of the Wilmot Public Library, give the librarian a two-week range of dates and a topic, and have her turn over a handful of yellow clippings from the *Wilmot Press Gazette* that would tell him what he needed to know.

But that's what had happened. Inside fifteen minutes he'd had five names, and it hadn't taken much review of the follow-up articles to decide that Marian Littlecross was the one he wanted to see.

He didn't expect an answer when he rang the bell beside the dull silver-framed screen door, and he didn't get one. Taking out one of his cards, he printed two sentences neatly on the back in blue felt-tip pen and wedged the card in between the door's frame and the grillwork decorating its front. The sentences read: "Ms. Littlecross: I have $55 for you if you have 15 minutes for me. I'll phone at 6:00."

On his way to the Red Roof Inn, where he had a reservation, he supplied himself with two bacon cheeseburgers, a large order of crispy curls, and a six-pack of beer. He figured that once he was in his room resting on pillows propped against the headboard of his bed, the food, the beer, and ESPN would just about get him through to six o'clock.

Gallagher had spent the better part of two hours the day before talking with Michaelson and Marjorie about the most effective way to approach the woman whose name he'd managed to find. The consensus was total deceit.

Gallagher didn't like that, particularly. On his office desk a Lucite paperweight encased a bromide in which he happened to believe with passionate intensity: "A Lie Doesn't Sell Anything But Your Competitor's Product." Unfortunately, though, he couldn't come up with anything within spitting distance of the truth that looked like it might work, so he was going along with the approach they'd suggested.

Promptly at six he muted the tube and called Littlecross's telephone number. He reached an answering machine. The voice on the recording sounded simultaneously defensive and world-weary. Gamely reminding himself of another piece of paperweight wisdom—"Selling Starts When the Customer Says No"—he took a deep breath and plunged in.

"Ms. Littlecross," he said after the beep, "this is Todd

Gallagher with SafeHome Security, and I've got some good news for you. Your name was selected for participation in a marketing survey that I'll be conducting for SafeHome in this area. The survey takes fifteen minutes flat, and your answers will of course be kept strictly confidential. If you're willing to take part, you'll be paid fifty-five dollars, and that's cash on the nail, before you answer question one. You can reach me—"

He stopped as he heard the phone pick up.

"Okay, I've heard enough," a husky contralto said.

"Ms. Littlecross?"

"That's me. I just wanted to hear what was behind the hint before I decided whether to talk to you. You checked out. The number on your card is the same one information has for your office in Raleigh, there's someone there who's heard of you, and the Better Business Bureau says you're reputable."

"I'm relieved to hear that," Gallagher said, reflecting automatically that this didn't sound like a woman who needed home security advice from him or anyone else.

"You gonna try to sell me anything? 'Cause I'll tell you right off the bat I'm not in the market. I have forty-five-caliber security, and that's all I've ever needed."

"No, ma'am, I'm not going to try to sell you a thing. I am a salesman and people tell me I'm good at it, but today I'm trying to get information that'll help me sell things to other people."

"I guess you might as well come on over, then. Just be sure you have the money, and plan on being out of here before *Seinfeld* comes on."

"See you in half an hour," Gallagher said.

★

The woman who opened her door to Gallagher twenty-seven minutes later looked as though she was in her early fifties. Light brown hair streaked with gray framed a square face with a no-nonsense, this-is-as-good-as-it's-gonna-get expression. The top of her head came almost to Gallagher's chin, which made her five-eight or five-nine, and that height deemphasized a solid build that would have appeared stocky on a shorter woman.

He gave her another of his cards and she invited him in. He stepped directly into a living room where a younger, thinner, shorter version of Marian Littlecross sat with her eyes fixed on a flickering television screen. She didn't glance up at Gallagher's entrance, and Gallagher looked at her only long enough to see her brush Dorito crumbs absently from an oversized, hot-pink T-shirt. Judging from her features, he would have said she was in her early twenties, although her posture, expression, and waist-length hair made him wonder if she were actually still an adolescent.

This would be the girl who, according to the clippings, had been rushed to the hospital with crudely bandaged wrists and a near-catatonic nervous breakdown after finding one of the praying-for-you-in-heaven cards in her mail. He hadn't thought that much about it, but seeing her there now, he shivered involuntarily at the thought of it. However obliquely, he could feel what it must have been like to read that card, without warning, a year after an abortion had ended the first and, as it turned out, the only pregnancy you'd ever have.

Apparently without considering an introduction, Marian Littlecross led Gallagher directly across the living room, through a small dining room, and into a brightly lit kitchen.

"I'm having coffee," she said as she gestured toward a

turquoise table and chairs against the far wall. "How about you?"

"Coffee would be fine, thanks. Black."

As Littlecross fussed with cups and a Mr. Coffee, Gallagher opened his Leatherette folder, pulled a standard survey form and a SafeHome logo envelope out of its cover pocket, and wondered exactly how he was going to bring this off. During the planning stage it had seemed as though getting in the door would be the hard part and the rest would be a snap: Just find a way to work Sharon Bedford's name into their chat, watch Littlecross's reaction, and make a judgment. Now that part didn't look like such a piece of cake after all.

Littlecross put a midnight blue mug at Gallagher's place and set a pearl gray mug at her own. Stark white lettering on each said BOREALIS HEALTH CENTER. Then she sat down and nodded at Gallagher with what he took to be permission to begin.

"First off," he said, handing her the envelope, "let's not forget your payment. You're kind enough to take time to talk to us, and we do appreciate it."

Littlecross slit the envelope open and examined its contents skeptically. She found a slick, full-color SafeHome brochure, a fifty, and a five. She folded the fresh-from-the-cash-machine currency into a pocket of her pale blue skirt and set the brochure and the envelope aside—both, obviously, destined for the trash the moment the door closed behind Gallagher.

Figuring that he'd purchased all the goodwill he was going to, Gallagher began going through the survey, asking questions that were carefully designed to make anyone answering them wonder whether they could stand to live another thirty minutes without a fully installed SafeHome security system: How many hours a day is the house empty? What percentage of the people in this neighborhood work away from home during the day? What did she think was the level of illegal drug use in Wilmot? Officials elsewhere estimated that over ninety percent of residential burglaries were committed by amateurs looking for things they could trade for drugs—did she think that was probably the situation in Wilmot as well?

And so on. Bored, monosyllabic answers. He was running out of time and questions and so far he didn't have a clue about how to get the only answer he cared about. Time for the punch line.

"We have a number of satisfied customers around the country who've given us permission to use their names in case you have any questions," he said. "In the Washington, D.C., area—Bethesda, Maryland, actually—there's Sharon Bedford."

He watched Littlecross's face. Nothing. Not a flicker.

"I thought you weren't going to try to sell me anything," she said.

"Absolutely right. Just in case you have any questions about the brochure."

This couldn't be it. All this way, all this time, all this effort for nothing but negative information. He'd come to believe in the connection between the Wilmot campaign ploy and Sharon's murder, and he wasn't ready to give up on it just because Marian Littlecross had a poker face. But he couldn't think of a way to push it any further.

His eyes scanned the modest kitchen in search of inspiration. Three rectangles—a plaque and two things in drugstore frames—hung on the twelve inches of wall above the sink, but he couldn't read any of them. Dish drainer, wall phone, an untidy pile of papers and address books. Nothing that sparked much of an idea.

Then he saw it. Perched sedately on top of the phone directories. A shiny green elephant, trunk curled, legs tucked under its baked-clay body, tusks jutting aggressively toward the sink. Taking up about two-thirds of the surface of the top book, the animal seemed massive.

"My word," Gallagher said, his voice filling with wonder. "Is that a *boo-fay*? I haven't seen one of those things in almost twenty-five years."

Boo-fay, as Gallagher correctly pronounced it, is an acronym spelled BUFE. The B stands for Big. The U stands for Ugly. The E stands for Elephant. About ninety percent of the BUFEs owned by Americans were bought in South Vietnam.

Littlecross looked quickly over her shoulder to follow Gallagher's eyes.

"Yeah, it is, matter of fact," she said. "It's been a long time since I've heard anyone call it that."

Rising, Gallagher crossed the room in two strides to examine the beast.

"Brings back memories," he muttered.

" 'Memories' is one word for them, I guess," Littlecross said.

What was the other? Gallagher wondered. *Nightmares*?

He looked up at the three hangings over the sink. The nearest was a Bachelor of Science in Nursing degree granted in 1967 by Duquesne University. A plaque, polished brass on dark pine, hung in the middle. Gallagher had read the bitter words engraved there before:

SOUTHEAST ASIA WAR GAMES
1965–1973
SECOND PLACE

The third hanging, beyond the plaque, was a photograph. Six impossibly young women with eyes impossibly old. They were all dressed in khaki uniforms. Four of them casually held cigarettes. Two were black and four were white. One of them was Marian Littlecross, many years ago. And although Gallagher knew the photograph Michaelson had seen only from Michaelson's detailed description, he realized instantly that another of the navy nurses in the picture before him was Deborah Moodie.

chapter

18

★

You have one new message," the electronic chirp reported
cheerfully. "Recorded at nine-twelve P.M."

"Uh-oh," Michaelson said, for it was now almost one A.M.

He had last checked his answering machine at nine. Then
he'd picked up Marjorie, not at Cavalier Books but at her
home. She'd had to leave the store early and change, because
they weren't just going out to a late dinner or the last showing
of a subtitled movie. They were going ballroom dancing at the
Austrian embassy.

With yesterday's rather ostentatious SafeHome LokBox de-
livery, Michaelson had decided it would be best to be away
from his apartment for the bulk of the next several evenings.
This had turned out to be a needless precaution yesterday
evening, when he'd returned bleary-eyed around three A.M. to
find that nothing had happened.

This morning, though—just barely, for the call came at
11:53—a longtime colleague had phoned from Foggy Bottom
with the news that warm bodies were needed this evening at
the Austrian embassy and a plea to pitch in for old times' sake.
He had agreed instantly, partly because of a weakness for the

older Strauss that he shared with Marjorie, but mostly because this sudden, custom-tailored invitation told him that tonight was The Night.

The orchestra played skillfully, the champagne sparkled, Michaelson's white dinner jacket gleamed lustrously under the chandeliers, Gallagher wasn't supposed to report until the next morning, and the (almost) carefree hours had slipped away.

Until now. Michaelson pressed 2 on the pay phone to trigger the message.

"Gallagher," a harried voice said. "I think I've stumbled on some big-time stuff that we'd better talk about real soon. As in yesterday. There aren't any more direct flights from Cleveland to Washington tonight, but there's a connection through Pittsburgh that should get me in a bit after midnight. I'll hop a cab over to your place, and if you're not back yet, I'll park outside your door till you show."

Michaelson glanced again at his watch. Twelve fifty-three.

"Problem?" Marjorie asked.

"Unless there's a highly unlikely backup on the Key Bridge, actually," Michaelson said, "this could be extremely unpleasant."

"It's a good thing we decided to take my car over here," Marjorie sighed. "Let's go."

Marjorie handed her car phone to Michaelson as her Chrysler Concord peeled up Fifteenth with a tire-squealing lurch. He'd given her the gist of Gallagher's message during their trot to the car.

"Call USAir at National and see if their flight from Pittsburgh got in on time," she instructed him.

"How do you know he's flying USAir?" Michaelson asked as he dialed information.

"I don't," she said. "It's just the only airline I can think of that flies from Pittsburgh."

Marjorie's educated guess proved right, and Michaelson had the information by the time Marjorie screeched through a red light at Massachusetts and P.

"The flight was somewhat delayed," he reported. "It reached the gate at twelve thirty-two."

"He won't have checked his bag," Marjorie muttered. "If he found a cabbie whose first language is English, this could be a dead heat."

They reached the Georgetown street where Michaelson lived at 1:03. Seeing neither a cab nor an ambulance, Marjorie slowed, cut her lights, and double-parked at the end of the block.

"This scene should be in black and white," she said. "I feel like I'm in a sixty-year-old Warner Brothers movie. Did you spot anyone?"

"No," Michaelson said, "but as John Wayne put it in *Fort Apache*, 'If you saw 'em, they weren't Apaches.' I'll guarantee you there's a lookout within sixty feet of my front door."

"Where are you going?" Marjorie demanded in some alarm as Michaelson began to get out of the car.

"I'm going to give the lookout something to see. Perhaps looking at a man standing outside his building to savor the night's memories for a few minutes will give the chap time to do his job and divert him from more mischievous pursuits."

"What if Gallagher already got here and is noisily pounding on your door?"

"Then we'll have to hope that our presumed visitors had a

backup plan more imaginative than simply coming out the front door."

"All right," Marjorie said. "I'll look for a parking space."

"Very well. But please don't come up until a light comes on in the window on the Wisconsin Avenue side."

Michaelson crossed the street deliberately as Marjorie pulled away, and upon reaching the opposite sidewalk, ambled without haste toward his apartment building. The white dinner jacket seemed absurdly conspicuous, but he would have felt exposed even in charcoal gray or navy blue. He reminded himself to suppress his sense of urgency, to stroll, not to hurry or do anything else that might spook someone a few yards away with a bad state of nerves on a hot summer night.

As he approached his building's entrance, he veered toward the street. Left hand in the side pocket of his pants. Right hand rubbing his nose, scratching his chin, dropping limply. He leaned forward and gazed down the street in each direction, as if hoping against hope that his companion might reconsider and return. He posed, imagining titles for the picture he was trying to create. *Too Early for Bed*, perhaps by Gibson. Or with a little wiggle in the brush strokes, *Night's Remnant* by one of the American Impressionists. His mind, meanwhile, sent urgent little telepathic messages into the shadows behind him: *You have plenty of time. No need to do anything rash.*

This went on for six minutes, which should have been more than ample. Turning deliberately, Michaelson then climbed toward the front door. It took him another thirty seconds to get into the lobby and call for the elevator. By the time he stepped from the elevator onto the fourth floor, there should have been abundant opportunity for any burglar not yet eligible for Social Security to get out the alley window and safely away.

He saw Gallagher pacing with nervous energy at the end of the hall, his suit carrier parked against the wall. A grin spreading across his face, Gallagher glanced up at him.

"I guess you got my message," he said.

"Only a few minutes ago when I called my answering machine," Michaelson said. "I've been at an embassy party all night and Ms. Randolph just dropped me off. Racing back to Washington in the small hours of the morning is above and beyond the call of duty, and flying USAir to do it was downright heroic."

"Maybe I got a little excited," Gallagher said. "But I thought what I found was pretty important, and I didn't want to get into it over the phone."

"Quite right. Well, let's go in, shall we?"

Michaelson raised the first of the two keys he'd normally need to get into his apartment. It was less than an inch from the lock when the door flew open. An instant later a hard right shoulder smashed into Michaelson's chest and sent him sprawling backward against Gallagher.

So much for imagination, Michaelson thought.

Michaelson felt himself being lowered gently to the floor. He saw the scampering burglar already at the opposite end of the hall, starting down the old-fashioned iron stairway there. Then, as he safely reached the floor, he felt Gallagher let go of him and saw the younger man hustle after the burglar.

"No!" Michaelson yelled, without the slightest discernible effect on Gallagher.

Michaelson scrambled to his feet and hurried after Gallagher and his prey, but he realized that he was doing it strictly for the exercise. This wasn't going to be any contest.

Football coaches distinguish between *fast* and *quick*. Gallagher was both, and by the time he burst out through the front door of Michaelson's building, the burglar had only a five- to ten-yard lead on him. As it happened, the burglar was at that point closing fast on Marjorie, who was approaching the entrance from the opposite direction. She stepped prudently aside.

Any doubts she had about what was going on evaporated when a dark-clad figure burst from the shadows beyond the steps and attempted to blindside Gallagher as he leaped from the entryway to the sidewalk.

The attempt was unsuccessful. Gallagher's left leg snapped viciously, the sole of his foot caught his attacker in the middle of his chest, and the man sprawled backward with a strangled groan. With the burglar's lead now slightly increased, Gallagher raced to continue his pursuit.

As Gallagher approached her, Marjorie did not step prudently aside. There are two things that can happen here, she thought, and both of them are bad.

"Down!" she yelled, making a grab for Gallagher's arm as he sprinted past her.

Gallagher ignored this injunction, but he didn't ignore the gunshot that whistled two feet over his head. He ducked in a wary squat behind the bumper of the nearest car, pulling Marjorie protectively with him.

"Get DOWN!" repeated Marjorie, whose idea of *down* where gunfire was concerned involved being prone.

Two more shots split the humid darkness. Glass shattered.

Sheet metal whined. Without further encouragement, Gallagher flattened himself on the street.

A pause. Long enough to raise your head, begin to tell your arms to push your body up.

Then three more shots, half a second apart. Fired from maybe a little farther away and a slightly different angle, but it was hard to be sure about that when you're busy kissing the bricks again. Wood splintered, a tire exploded, and stone screamed with a ricochet.

Another pause, this one shorter. Then more shots. Too many, fired too fast to have any hope of counting them. But those were just fireworks anyway. Neither Gallagher nor Marjorie had any intention of raising their heads until the gunner had had plenty of time to leave the area in the privacy he clearly desired.

Their first impulse when they finally did look up sixty seconds later was to glance back at where the guy who'd tried to tackle Gallagher had landed after Gallagher's drop-kick. He was gone.

"Joker had tried anything that lame with Victor Charlie, he'd've come home in a body bag," Gallagher said. Unused adrenaline still pumping through his body made his voice ragged.

"The rules are slightly milder in nineties Georgetown," Marjorie said. "Though not too much milder, apparently."

Gallagher glanced back in the direction the shots had come from.

"That son of a gun emptied a clip at us," he said.

"He emptied a clip," Marjorie said, "but he managed to hit everything in the neighborhood except us. We just learned something important."

★

Well," Gallagher said as he examined the open and empty SafeHome LokBox still nestled in Michaelson's kitchen cabinet, "I guess we'll have to pay off on the guarantee."

"Oh, I don't think it was really a fair test," Michaelson said. "They obviously had someone keeping an eye on me by the time your safe was delivered. They knew what they were up against and they came prepared."

"Who's 'they'?" Gallagher asked.

"I'm still working on that one," Michaelson said.

It was 1:45 A.M. Marjorie was tending a pot of coffee. Michaelson was tending a stoveful of scrambled eggs, bacon, sausage, and toast, for hearing fifteen gunshots and having none of them hit you produces a thoroughly existential disregard for the preoccupations of AMA spoilsports. Michaelson piled hot, cholesterol-laden food onto a platter, which he set on the table in the midst of an eclectic array of knives, forks, and plates.

"After you've had a bite," Michaelson said genially to Gallagher, "why don't you tell me what you found in Ohio?"

Gallagher spent six minutes making eggs and breakfast

meat disappear and four describing the fruits of his trip to Wilmot. Michaelson listened, sober and surprised, to a clipped, precise rundown of information he hadn't expected.

"We sent you to Ohio to look for information that doesn't exist," he said quietly, "and you came back with a key answer we were supposed to be searching for in Washington."

"Why Deborah Moodie revived her crusade on the Artemus/favoritism issue, you mean?" Gallagher asked.

"Yes."

"Revived it in early 'ninety-three," Marjorie said, "which happens to have been during the transition between the outgoing and incoming administrations. Probably not a coincidence."

"Probably not," Michaelson agreed wryly. "I suspect that Ms. Moodie was moved to revisit the issue when she learned that Jeffrey Quentin was going to hold a lot of power in the new administration."

"And why should that have bothered her?" Marjorie asked. "I mean, apart from the reasons that it bothered everyone."

"We've now reached the stage of informed speculation," Michaelson said.

"Is that a fancy way of saying you're making it up?" Gallagher asked.

"I'll give you my theory and you be the judge," Michaelson said.

"Fair enough."

"Facts first," Michaelson said. "One: Deborah Moodie and Marian Littlecross served as nurses in the same unit in Vietnam. Two: Jeffrey Quentin some twenty years later caused Littlecross's daughter terrible emotional and psychological pain by using her as a pawn in a congressional campaign.

Inference: Ms. Moodie found out about that when Ms. Lit-tlecross turned to her and other old friends for support in her emotional crisis. This isn't some bloodless violation of a sub-paragraph in a protocol somewhere, like the general's relative getting favored treatment. This is real and immediate pain, inflicted on the daughter of someone who had a special bond with Moodie."

"I'm with you," Gallagher said. "If someone had done what Quentin did to the daughter of a guy who served in the same platoon I did, I'd've killed the son of a bitch with my bare hands. Begging your pardon, Ms. Randolph."

"I've heard the term before," Marjorie said. "In this context I don't think any other word would quite do."

"Deborah Moodie apparently didn't view homicide as an option," Michaelson said, "but she had to be deeply alarmed by the prospect of Jeffrey Quentin holding major power in the government of the United States. And she had to be even more deeply alarmed by something else."

"I'll bite," Marjorie said. "What?"

"Her suspicion, or her certain knowledge, that in Jerry Marciniak's quest for power he had worked with Quentin before. The identities of women who undergo abortions are highly confidential. For Quentin's congressional campaign ploy to work, he had to get the names from somewhere. The director of the National Medical Records Compilation, Data Collection and Privacy Concerns Bureau—which is what Marciniak happened to be at a critical point—is a distinctly plausible source."

"Definitely speculation," Marjorie said.

"Artemus was already out long before 'ninety-three. There was no reason to start going after him again. But we know that as the prospect of Quentin reaching power loomed, Deborah Moodie launched a desperate effort to revive a charge that might derail Marciniak's career. She must have known that her attempt would almost certainly prove futile. If she went ahead, it had to be because she believed that Marciniak was evil, that allowing him to get the kind of power he could hope for with Quentin's patronage was unacceptable, and that morally she simply had to try to stop him."

"In early 1993," Marjorie said thoughtfully, "half this town would have given you five-to-three odds that within eighteen months a federal bureaucrat would be running the entire U.S. health-care system."

"And Deborah Moodie could plausibly have feared that that bureaucrat would be Jerry Marciniak," Michaelson said.

"You keep saying 'could have,' " Gallagher said. "I guess that's why you called it a theory."

"Well, there are a couple more things we know," Michaelson said. "We know Ms. Moodie did try to revive the issue. We know that she got squashed. We know that Scott Pilkington knew why she got squashed. And we know that Pilkington's working with Quentin. That much is more than theory."

"We know another fact, too," Gallagher said wearily. "We know that the bad guys have the written order now."

"They, ah, don't, actually," Michaelson said, with what in anyone else would have been a suggestion of embarrassment at having kept Gallagher in the dark about part of his plans.

"Where is it, then?"

"It's on the back of the writing table over there, in the same envelope as my electric bill."

"You mean you never put the written order in the safe?" Gallagher demanded.

"Oh, I put it in there initially," Michaelson assured him. "But once I was sure they were coming after the thing, it seemed silly to leave it in the first place they'd look. So I took it out."

"So after breaking into your apartment and rifling that lockbox, those jokers have nothing but air to show for it?" Gallagher asked, chortling.

"Not quite nothing," Michaelson said. "After removing the original order, I stocked the safe with a photocopy, inside a white envelope, and annotated with a brief message."

"The point of all that being what?" Gallagher asked.

"To find out who killed Sharon Bedford. That's the part of this I actually care about. All this talk about treason is quite soul-stirring, but as Talleyrand pointed out, treason is generally just a question of dates. Sharon Bedford was a human being."

A few moments of thoughtful silence followed. Then Gallagher spoke.

"I'm slow," he said quietly. "I'm not quite following how writing a note on a copy of the order gets us to Sharon's killer. Can you sorta run your thinking past me at submedium speed?"

"Sharon Bedford's murder was a Washington crime," Michaelson said. "It was committed by a Washington killer for a reason that only makes sense in Washington terms. Businessmen and loan sharks kill to conceal crimes, stockbrokers and union officers kill for useful information, husbands and wives and street thugs kill for money. But Sharon Bedford couldn't have been killed by anyone like that, for any of those reasons. If we want to find her killer, we have to focus on Washington players following Washington rules."

The phone rang. Without getting out of his chair, Michael-son reached back, unhooked the receiver, and brought it to his ear.

"Very funny," the voice at the other end barked.

"Why, Scott," Michaelson said. "We were just talking about you."

Michaelson told Pilkington that they couldn't meet until two o'clock that afternoon. The excuse he offered was that, having politely given Pilkington's burglars until the small hours of the morning to get their work done, he now intended to sleep late, and any conferences would have to be scheduled around his body's demand for rest. While there was something to this, the more important reason for the delay was that before talking to Pilkington, Michaelson and Marjorie each needed to make a phone call.

★

Michaelson's call went to the Moodies' residence. He made it at 7:45 A.M., before either Alex or Deborah would have left for work. They both got on the line, Alex in the kitchen and Deborah in the den.

"Marian Littlecross sends her regards, figuratively speaking," Michaelson began.

"Thanks, figuratively speaking," Deborah said. "How did you find her?"

"I found her by having someone read the newspapers. I discovered her connection with you by accident."

"So?" Deborah said then, after a pause. The syllable was tentative and defensive rather than challenging.

Michaelson explained the part of his theory linking Deborah's revival of the Artemus favoritism issue to a suspicion on her part that Marciniak had helped Quentin and fear of what that might mean once Quentin acquired real power. This took about a minute. Neither of the Moodies interrupted him or asked any questions.

"It's a theory," he said, "and a rather speculative theory at that. I'm talking to Scott Pilkington in about six hours and I need you to confirm the theory, if it's right, before I do."

A heavy silence lasting ten to fifteen painful seconds followed. Finally Deborah Moodie spoke.

"I don't feel I can discuss this with you," she said, her voice distant and her words a trifle clipped.

"I understand," Michaelson said, having just received the confirmation he needed. "Then perhaps you can tell me something a bit more specific about bufotenine than Pilkington shared with me when he discussed the results of Ms. Bedford's autopsy."

The tone of Deborah's voice as she answered suggested that it was a vast relief to have the conversation shift from a personal to a professional plane.

"I'm not an expert or anything, but I can give you a broad outline," she said. "It's a fairly well-known poison, derived from frog-gland secretions or something like that."

"Fatal if ingested orally, even if it doesn't get into the bloodstream?" Michaelson asked.

"Should be. I think it can be absorbed in fatal dosages even through mucous membranes, without being swallowed at all."

"Thank you," Michaelson said. Again.

Marjorie's call went to Hilda Ashley, a career civil servant who had recently found a niche as administrative assistant to the deputy head of the State Department's Management Information Services Bureau, or MIS. A relatively new office, MIS had yet to win even grudging respect from veteran foreign service officers. Some crusty FSOs had acquired the habit of summoning MIS operatives by telling their secretaries to "call Nerd Central and tell them to send up a propeller-head."

Hilda Ashley was quite ambitious by civil service standards, had thin skin and a long memory, and spent just under a thousand dollars a year on books. Marjorie called her a few minutes after 10:30 A.M., when she was sure that Ashley would be back from her morning coffee break.

"Hilda," she said, "I'm calling because I have one last autographed copy of *Ties That Bind* by Warren Adler left, and it might sell at any moment."

"Thank you, but I've already read it."

"I remember selling you your copy," Marjorie said. "I wanted to let you know about this autographed one because a mischievous soul who swore me to secrecy suggested that the MIS Bureau might want to give a copy as a gift to one or more deserving FSOs."

This was a lie but a safe one, given the interest of MIS in general and Hilda Ashley in particular in subtly embarrassing any number of foreign service officers. Would one or two of those gents, to Ashley's knowledge, find it disconcertingly suggestive to be presented with a mystery novel set in Washington, featuring a woman who acts out sadomasochistic fantasies with a high-government official? That was one of the world's safer bets.

"The idea does have a certain appeal, at that," Ashley said. "I'll keep it in mind."

"Actually," Marjorie said, "Richard is popping over to see Scott Pilkington this afternoon around two, and I'm meeting him there so that we can go on to a late lunch afterward. If you like, I could leave the book with you on sort of a consignment basis. If you and your chums at MIS like the idea, you can pass the hat and send me a check when you get around to it. If you don't think it's worth the trouble, I'll just pick the book back up the next time I'm in the neighborhood."

"I don't see how I can turn that down," Ashley said. "I'll see you when you get here."

Marjorie and Michaelson reached the State Department several minutes early. Getting beyond the ground-floor guard station at the State Department requires a pass for a specific location. Visitors don't wander the halls seeking chance acquaintances and familiar faces. Accordingly, Marjorie waited with Michaelson in a comfortable secretarial area outside Pilkington's office. Pilkington's secretary left word with Ashley's that Marjorie was there, on the off chance that Ashley might want to drop by.

She did. Before she did, Kenneth Lytton Denzell passed through the area and spoke for a few moments with Pilkington's secretary.

Marjorie suspected that this wasn't happenstance. Kenneth Lytton Denzell was Assistant Secretary of State for International Policy Issues. He was a political appointee, with a tenure at the State Department directly proportional to the residence of the current incumbent at the White House. Marjorie had expected Denzell to hear from Hilda Ashley who Pilkington's visitors this afternoon would be, and apparently he had. She now expected Jeffrey Quentin to hear the same thing from Denzell.

Denzell had been gone about two minutes when Pilkington emerged from his office, shook hands warmly with Michaelson and Marjorie, graciously invited Michaelson into his office, and pointedly did not include Marjorie in the invitation. Marjorie sat back down in the waiting area and opened a book—not, as it happened, *Ties That Bind*, which she'd already read.

"So," Pilkington said, "you have it."

"Obviously. And the next time someone tries to take it away from me, it's going straight to the *Washington Post*."

"Any doubt about its authenticity?"

"None."

"Name your price," Pilkington said, a frown of distaste at the uncharacteristically direct words spoiling his face for a moment.

"The head of Sharon Bedford's murderer, on a silver platter. Let me hasten to add that I'm speaking metaphorically."

"I'll interpret your metaphor as comprehending something consistent with due process of law. The fact remains that I don't know who Sharon Bedford's murderer is."

"Neither do I," Michaelson said.

"Then how am I supposed to deliver?"

"I've given that matter considerable thought," Michaelson said. "I've come up with an easy way and a hard way."

"I suppose the easy way involves bugging the telephones

and eavesdropping electronically on the offices of one or more government officials," Pilkington sighed.

"Yes."

"That would be a felony."

"You view that as a decisive objection, I take it?" Michaelson asked.

"I do."

"I suppose I should be a bit miffed that quibbles like that didn't prove so inhibiting when the issue was a black-bag operation targeting my apartment."

"That was *not* a black-bag operation," Pilkington interjected quickly. "That was a one-hundred-percent legal search carried out pursuant to a warrant based on duly attested probable cause to believe that evidence of violation of federal statutes governing dissemination of classified documents would be discovered."

"I don't suppose the magistrate who signed that warrant has formed the impression that he has a direct shot at the next Supreme Court vacancy, has he?"

"Not my department," Pilkington said. "I handle the policy end of things."

"At any rate," Michaelson said, "that leaves the hard way."

"Describe it to me."

Michaelson did.

"I hate it," Pilkington said when Michaelson had finished.

"I'm not crazy about it myself."

"I can't go along with it. The risks are too great. The game isn't worth the candle."

"You don't have any choice but to go along with it," Michaelson said. "If you slam the door in my face, leaks, hints, winks, and nudges about the coup d'état order start forty-five minutes after I leave your office."

"Regrettable but, bottom line, I can live with that," Pilkington said.

"Please don't interrupt me in the middle of my threat," Michaelson said. "You see, while Marjorie Randolph and I were cooling our heels outside your office, Kenneth Denzell passed through."

"What a stunning coincidence," Pilkington said. He looked as if he'd just sipped from a glass of Mouton Cadet '83 with which some perverse sommelier had mixed Diet Coke.

"Quentin will get Denzell's report, and when the leaks start, Quentin will conclude that you're putting the information out, using me as a cat's paw. He'll assume that instead of trying to get the document from me, as you've been truthfully telling him you're doing, you in fact passed the document to me, using Marjorie as a cutout—you know, left a photocopy on your secretary's desk where Marjorie could see it while you and I were in here chatting, that kind of thing."

"I am familiar with the term 'cutout,' " Pilkington said frostily.

"Anyhow," Michaelson concluded with an eloquent shrug, "you've been running for him all this time because he looked like the best bet you had, but all your efforts go down the drain if I decide to go to the scribblers. The only way to keep Quentin from thinking that you're double-crossing him is to double-cross him."

Wrapping his right hand around his chin, Pilkington studied the lower left quadrant of his desk intently for nearly a minute. Then he looked back up and met Michaelson's gaze.

"I dislike this intensely," he said.

"Yes. Well, it's a filthy job, but someone has to do it, don't they?"

chapter

21

★

Michaelson's proposal to Pilkington had three parts. Michaelson and Gallagher began the first one late that afternoon.

They returned to Sharon Bedford's apartment, arriving just before five P.M. Gallagher turned the alarm off and they went inside. They stayed inside for forty-five minutes, more than long enough to install a SafeHome LokBox in the cabinet above her refrigerator. They left the lockbox open and the cabinet door ajar.

Michaelson returned to Gallagher's Cadillac. After he was sure that Michaelson had had time to get back to the car, Gallagher turned the apartment alarm back on, exited the apartment, closed the door, and locked it. He waited one more minute. Then, without turning the alarm off, he unlocked the door, pushed it open, and walked away.

Forty-five seconds later a siren began screaming from the apartment. Gallagher by this time had reached the sidewalk. He continued along it without haste for another ten seconds, slipped into the front seat of his car beside Michaelson, and drove off.

Four minutes and five seconds later a Montgomery County

Police Department patrol car pulled up outside the town-house complex. Two and a half hours or so after that, Patrolman Steph Richardson submitted a written report detailing his discovery of a concealed but open and empty safe in Bedford's apartment, and his failure to find any other indication of mischief on the part of whoever had triggered the alarm.

Although the following morning was a Saturday, a copy of Richardson's report, summarized and annotated by Pilkington, landed on Quentin's desk at eleven A.M.

The second phase was a bit more complicated. Evidence of it didn't surface until ten days later.

That evidence took the form of three paragraphs in a *Washington Post* article on the future of American intelligence agencies in the post–Cold War world. Starting at the top of the article's second column, the first of the three paragraphs noted that a proposal to establish a "permanent task force" on coordination of intelligence-gathering activities had suddenly advanced from something everyone had had at the back of his credenza for five years to something that was about to happen in a big hurry.

The next paragraph opined that, particularly in light of the Aldrich Ames/Soviet mole fiasco, this embryonic task force had all the earmarks of an outfit intended to gather all intelligence responsibility under a single new directorate, leaving the CIA with Operations and Hardware Maintenance.

The final paragraph, amid references to "senior officials" and other allusions to deep background chats, mentioned four candidates for the task force chairmanship: two who were clearly impossible, one who would have accepted a caustic enema before taking an appointment from the incumbent president, and Richard Michaelson.

" 'Permanent task force.' There's a nice Washington touch," the deputy director of the Central Intelligence Agency said when he saw the story. The CIA has heard the permanent task force rumor roughly once every eighteen months for forty years and no longer pays much attention to it.

Lacking this institutional memory, Jeffrey Quentin reacted with less equanimity. He called several senior officials and demanded acidly whether they planned on telling the president whom he'd be inviting into his administration before they made it official. The responses varied from veiled condescension to borderline derision—unsubtle reminders that the people Quentin was talking to were the permanent government, whereas Quentin himself was as good as out of town.

Except for Scott Pilkington's response. Pilkington, who at least paid lip service to the respect that Quentin's position should in theory have commanded, analyzed the development with his customary lucidity when Quentin phoned him. Deconstructing the *Post* story and putting it together with the police report, Pilkington accompanied Quentin effortlessly to the conclusion that Michaelson must have come up with a hard copy of the coup d'état order and was now capitalizing on it.

"So you're saying for sure he has the goods," Quentin said.

"That's the way it looks from here," Pilkington said with long-practiced, big-picture expansiveness.

"And he's showing them to everyone in town except us."

"That's definitely the implication."

"We can't keep leaving the initiative to him, goddammit," Quentin snapped. "We have to get proactive on this. We've gotta smoke him out."

"Perhaps," Pilkington said judiciously. "Or perhaps we should use him to smoke someone else out."

"Marciniak?"

"He's the only other player I know who seems to have one of the damn things."

"I *know* that," Quentin said sardonically. "I told *you* that, and I told you how he got it. But he's been guarding it like the crown jewels for years. What can we do with Michaelson to change Marciniak's mind?"

"Marciniak's been guarding his duplicate original of the order because he wants to use it one more time, at exactly the right moment, to get the one thing he really wants."

"Agreed. So what?"

"Marciniak's crown jewel loses one hundred percent of its value overnight if Michaelson decides to make his public," Pilkington explained. "By turning it over to you, for example."

"By God, I think you've got something," Quentin said, his voice softening to a near whisper and quickening with excitement. "If we let Marciniak know that Michaelson has the same bombshell he does, find a way to really rub his nose in it, then make him think Michaelson's in the process of auctioning it off, he's gonna have to take the damn thing out of whatever hole he's put it in and make the best deal he can with it. Right now. And I'll have every goddamn ace at the table."

"There's an outside-the-Beltway foreign policy conference in about three months at Hilton Head," Pilkington began almost dreamily. "I was thinking—"

"Screw your conference," Quentin yelped. "Screw your three months. I haven't got any three goddamn months. Get

Marciniak a copy of that police report before lunch, and make sure he understands what it means."

"Consider it done," Pilkington said, just the hint of an edge to his voice. "I mentioned the Hilton Head conference because it seems to me that someone in line to chair a permanent task force ought to have a key organizational role at a conference like that. He should pop down there on the government's nickel in the next week or so, talk to the on-scene people, make some security assessments, walk over the grounds, kick the tires, that kind of thing."

"So?"

"He'll need some input from your end, of course."

"You bet your ass," Quentin said, beginning to understand.

"On the other hand, we can't have the White House openly involved. You'd want to have some innocuous agency reserve the rooms and clear the bills."

"What agency did you have in mind?"

"Jerry Marciniak's," Pilkington said. "That way, he'll know that Michaelson and you were both going to be down at Hilton Head, with every chance in the world to get chummy and make deals. Marciniak's a smart chap. You did mention rubbing his nose in it, didn't you?"

A tense, electric silence throbbed over the line for five seconds while Quentin calmed himself and tumbled in stages to the elegant, delicately nuanced beauty of the idea. Then he spoke.

"Do it," he snapped.

Pilkington hung up, beating Quentin's click by a quarter-second or so. The third phase of Michaelson's proposal was under way.

★

I'm not certain the second reservation is in my name," Michaelson told the desk clerk at the Hilton Head Radisson four days later. "It may be under the National Health Research Agency."

"Yes, here it is," the smiling young woman said. "That room has already been registered. Two-oh-four, right next to yours."

She turned to the bank of pigeonholes behind her and took a cardboard folder from the 204 slot.

"Your name is on that folder, too, so I guess I'll just give it to you," she said.

"That will be fine," Michaelson said, accepting the second cardboard folder and palming it underneath the one he'd already been given for his own room.

He glanced inside. His folder held two rectangular plastic key-cards, as he'd requested. The folder for 204 held one key. Strolling across the lobby, he tossed the folder for 204 to Jeffrey Quentin.

"We might as well start by looking at the rooms," he said. "They're only on the second floor. Let's just take the stairs."

"Fine," Quentin sighed, heaving himself out of an overstuffed chair.

"Do you have any searing insights to share with me so far in your capacity as an expert consultant?" Michaelson asked as they walked together toward the stairway.

"Sure," Quentin muttered. "Get receipts for everything and don't pimp for anyone lower on the food chain than sub-committee chair."

They found Rooms 202 and 204 at the right end of the second-floor hallway. Michaelson opened 202, which looked like a double room, almost suite-sized. They stepped inside and glanced around.

"They tell me they can move the bed and the dresser out, put some more tables and chairs in, and we can use this for the conference nerve center," Michaelson said.

"Makes sense. I don't envy whoever ends up with the room next door when the conference actually happens, but I guess that's not your problem."

"Actually, I'll probably take it myself to preserve the illusion that I'm at the heart of the action," Michaelson said with a hint of self-mockery. "You can give me a report on it after tonight. That should be at least as productive a way for us to spend the public's dollars as sipping gin and tonics and looking at pretty girls in string bikinis will be—and that's close to the next thing on the agenda for this little boon-doggle."

"Look at it this way," Quentin said. "We'll be spending the money more wisely than the taxpayers would if we let them keep it."

Walking over to the adjoining door between the suite and Quentin's room, Michaelson slid the metal sleeve on the chest-level tongue-and-groove lock back and forth across its tracks. Then he ambled to the windows and checked their locks in the same desultory way.

"Security inspection is complete," he said offhandedly. "I can't think of any good reason to put off my examination of the patio bar and the poolside view any longer. My meeting with the arrangements manager isn't for another two hours yet. Care to join me in, say, forty-five minutes?"

"Knock on my door," Quentin said, and stepped toward his own room.

A hustling bellhop, spotless in summer whites, appeared a couple of minutes later with the bags for both rooms. Michaelson tipped him two dollars, as prescribed by executive-branch travel guidelines, and began to unpack. He hadn't quite finished when he heard the rap on his door.

"Dr. Marciniak," he said as he opened the door. "What a surprise. Please come in."

Jerry Marciniak stepped briskly into the room, tossing a New York Mets baseball cap on the bed. He strode to the window bank on the far side of the room, then turned to face Michaelson.

"Thank you for reserving and then registering the rooms, by the way," Michaelson said. "Surely you didn't have to fly down yourself to take care of that chore, though, did you?"

"I take every perk I can get," Marciniak said. "I know jobs that'd pay me three times what the government does. I'm not complaining, but this kind of thing is part of the deal. When the eagle flies, I go along for the ride."

"Well, I hope you enjoy your stay as much as I intend to enjoy mine," Michaelson said. "Anything in particular I can do for you?"

"Sorry to be abrupt, but I don't really have time for foreplay on this one. Have you given it to him yet?"

" 'It' being the order? He wouldn't be here if I had, and I'm no more likely than you are to tuck it into a travel bag and haul it to a hotel room."

"Good," Marciniak said, pacing around the expansive room. "Then there's still time for us to help each other instead of screwing each other."

"The ball's in your court," Michaelson said with a chilly, make-it-good smile.

"We need to level with each other," Marciniak said. "If we let him play one of us off against the other, he'll win and both of us will lose."

"That's a view I've held for some time, actually," Michaelson said.

"What has Quentin offered you for your duplicate original of the order?"

"The moon, the stars, and the sky," Michaelson said. "What has he offered you for yours?"

"Assuming I actually have one," Marciniak said.

"You have one," Michaelson said genially. "Only a handful of people had them, one of them got a favor only you could provide, and a short time later you achieved a dramatic promotion."

"That might have been charm and good looks," Marciniak said, grinning.

"If your abundant talent were enough, you would've become a senior policy-maker long ago. I thought we were playing straight with each other, by the way."

"Fair enough," Marciniak said. "I have one, Quentin's offered me a blank check, and so far I haven't delivered. But apparently he thinks that you will."

"Why do you say that?" Michaelson asked. "Because of my chairmanship of a Gilbert-and-Sullivan task force that some reporter thinks is going to replace half the CIA?"

"Yes," Marciniak said. "Because of that. Plus, with apologies to Rodgers and Hammerstein, because of things I've heard from fellas who were talking like they know."

"The fact is he's far from sure that I will come across with the order," Michaelson said. "This little task force flutter is his idea of an appetizer. To taste the main course, he's made it clear that I have to put a hard-copy duplicate original of the critical order in his hands."

"I'd say you're tempted."

"Sorely," Michaelson admitted. "As you must be. I frankly would have expected you to succumb to your temptation long ago, before I was even in the picture. Your self-restraint to date borders on inspirational."

"Self-restraint has nothing to do with it," Marciniak said. He stopped pacing and, affecting a nonchalant pose, leaned against the locked door joining the two rooms, slipping his hands into his pockets. "I've told him what I want, but I've also told him I'm not sure his boss will ever be in a position to deliver it. The position I want doesn't exist yet, and I'm not sure Quentin's going to be a player when it does."

"You want to be health policy czar, when and if the federal government takes over the financing of medical care in this country—is that a pretty fair guess?" Michaelson asked.

"Except there's no 'if' about it. You've got half the fat cats in the country paying eight thousand, ten thousand a year for health insurance for themselves already, and going up by three percent a quarter. Plus what they pay for their employees. It can't go on. I don't care which party has a majority in Congress or who wins the presidential elections. I don't care if conservatives or liberals or the Christian right or the radical left end up calling the shots. Ideological purity stops when the checkbooks come out. It's simple arithmetic. What we have now simply cannot continue. It's going to change. The change may be packaged and labeled as something else, but the federal government's going to be functionally running health care in this country before any of us gets too much older."

"And when that happens," Michaelson prompted, "you want to be running the show."

"You bet I do," Marciniak said. "Deputy Director for Health Policy. I told Quentin it had to be a quasi-tenured office, like the Director of the FBI. Seven-year term, Senate confirmation, dismissal only for cause, budget subject to independent congressional authorization."

"At least you didn't demand cabinet-level status."

"Only a moron would care about cabinet-level *status*," Marciniak said, whipping out his right hand and jabbing the air with his index finger. "I want cabinet-level *power*. Let the Secretary of Health and Human Services walk point. That's fine with me—as long as she signs the checks and stays out of my shop."

Marciniak's eyes shone as this torrent of words flowed. Michaelson met the passionate verbal onslaught with a jovial and almost condescending smile.

"You've obviously thought this through thoroughly," he said mildly. "I'm sure your course is a wise one."

"Except it all goes south if you get greedy," Marciniak said.

"I don't think I'm the one who sounds greedy," Michaelson protested. "I haven't asked for a fully autonomous, quasi-tenured appointment yet."

"That's not what I mean," Marciniak said, spitting the words out in a short, impatient burst. "We each have something very valuable. Agreed?"

"Obviously."

"Now, there's two ways we can each use our little asset.

There are people still in powerful positions who want that order kept secret. Certainly through the next election and, depending on who ends up on each ticket, probably well beyond that. We can take what they'll give us in exchange for keeping it secret. On the other hand, there are people like Quentin who want that order made public, and we can take what they'll give us for letting them publicize it."

"It's hard to argue with any of that," Michaelson said, a bit dismissively.

"The thing is, you can *threaten* to disclose the order an indefinite number of times. It's as worthwhile the tenth time as the first."

"You apparently speak from experience, to which I defer," Michaelson said.

"But you can only *actually* disclose it once," Marciniak said insistently. "As soon as it shows up above the fold on the front page of the *Washington Post,* no one cares about any threats to reveal it again. You've shot your wad. From that day forward, the asset's worth zero. Mine *and* yours."

"Fair enough. Your point, I take it, is that you and I can make a gentlemen's agreement, and as long as we trust each other and respect that agreement, we can by our forbearance preserve the value of the documentary proof that we share."

"Exactly."

"Of course," Michaelson said, "the value of our document diminishes over time. As late as 1992 this would certainly have been a huge story. Today, as you pointed out, it would still stir very great interest. But every year the number of powerful people who could be compromised or inconvenienced if this came out goes down. Combine that with the fact that either you or I might prove untrustworthy, and the risk of sitting on the order increases exponentially over time. If I were Quentin, I'd suggest to you—and to me—that the best thing to do now is to get the maximum immediate value that we can for the thing with a onetime disclosure."

"By giving it to him, you mean?"

"Yes."

"You sound like he's already made that pitch to you."

"He hasn't," Michaelson said. "At least in those words. But he will. And he'll also make it to you."

"Suppose I cross my heart and promise to say no?" Marciniak asked with a biting smile.

"That would satisfy me just as much as an equivalent performance by me would satisfy you," Michaelson said. "No, I think we'll need something a bit more concrete. Safe-deposit box requiring two keys, something like that. But this will all be academic unless we both resist temptation this weekend. Quentin is here, and as you've already pointed out, he's going to spend his time playing each of us off against the other. If neither of us sells out, we'll have something to talk about on Monday. If both of us do, then we'll both lose."

"How about if one does and the other doesn't?"

"Then one of us will be a victim and the other a fool," Michaelson said. "We have no choice but to trust each other until we're both back in Washington. No bargain with Quentin can be relied on without ironclad guarantees in place. There's no way he can give those to either of us this weekend."

Marciniak moved away from the adjoining door and gave Michaelson an intrigued and appraising gaze as he walked over to the hallway door.

"Quentin and I will be sipping gin and tonics by the patio bar in the very near future," Michaelson said. "If it would make you feel more secure, you'd be welcome to join us."

"That's all right," Marciniak said. "I can't keep tabs on you for the entire weekend, any more than you can keep an eye on me. I'm going to freshen up, hit CNN for half an hour, and return phone calls. I'm in six-fifteen if something comes up."

"Until later, then," Michaelson said.

He finished unpacking, reknotted his bow tie, washed his hands, and stepped into the corridor to knock on Quentin's door. Quentin joined him immediately, and they walked downstairs together in search of alcoholic refreshment and female visual relief.

With Michaelson's professorial reserve and Quentin's nervous, hustler's energy, they stood out among the vacationing lawyers, executives, award-winning salespeople, and small-business owners populating the patio bar. Someone with binoculars in Room 615, for example, could have spotted them without difficulty.

The hotel operator confirmed later that, in response to calls from a house phone rather than a room phone, she rang 202 and 204 twenty times each a few minutes after Michaelson and Quentin reached the patio bar.

Three minutes after that, the lock on Room 204's hallway door clicked and Marjorie Randolph heard the door begin to swing cautiously open. She was sitting fully clothed in the bathtub at the time, and had been feeling quite ridiculous. At the ominous lock-clicks a healthy fear replaced all other feelings, for she suspected that a murderer was about to pass six feet or so from her.

From behind the shower curtain in the darkened bathroom, she heard the door close. The entrant walked quietly on thick carpet, and she heard only an occasional shuffle, not regular footsteps. Then, from well inside the room, she heard metal sliding on metal, followed by the kind of squeak that comes from a seldom-used hinge.

She spent five seconds gathering her courage. After all, she told herself, she had a perfectly plausible explanation to offer the intruder, if she was discovered. Unless, of course, the intruder was Quentin. In which case, she thought, I can just kick his teeth in.

She rose slowly and stepped barefoot onto the bathroom floor. The rustle of the shower curtain as she did so sounded to her like surf pounding on the shore. She stepped cautiously to the bathroom door and, after a heart-stopping pause, looked out in each direction. She couldn't see anyone else in Quentin's room. And the door joining it to Room 202 was open.

Moving a bit more boldly now, she crossed to the adjoining door. She waited until she was sure the sound of movement through the doorway came from the closet area, well away from where she'd be standing.

As quietly as she could manage, she slipped Room 204's adjoining door closed and slid the metal lock home on its grooves. Scurrying to the phone beside the bed, she dialed a number that had been pounding her head for ten minutes.

"Patio bar," a genial Southern voice said after one ring. After inaudible mumbles the voice said, "You looking for someone named Michaelson?"

"Yes," Marjorie said.

"Michaelson here," was the next thing she heard.

"Scramble," she said. And hung up.

★

The first thing Michaelson saw when he opened the door to his room less than two minutes later was a look of sharp and unpleasant aggravation on Marciniak's face. Marciniak was standing at the closed and stubbornly unyielding adjoining door at the time, so the expression was understandable.

"How does that hoary old joke go?" Michaelson asked innocently. " 'No, madam, *I* am surprised. *You* are astonished.' I'm tempted to feed you the straight line just so you can use the riposte on me."

"Side-splitting, tiger, just side-splitting," Marciniak said. "All right, you got me. I wasn't certain you were telling the truth when you said you didn't have the order with you down here. I wanted to make sure before I gave you all weekend to cut a deal behind my back."

Michaelson stepped the rest of the way into his room, trailed by Quentin and Marjorie. Flipping the lights on as he came, he crossed all the way to a round work table by the windows. Quentin stayed in between Marciniak and the hallway door, while Marjorie perched primly on the edge of the bed.

"You ought to be more careful with the keys to your room," Quentin said to Michaelson.

"No, you should be more careful with the keys to yours. It's the locks I should be more careful with."

"You're being elliptical, Richard," Marjorie said. "Perhaps you should explain in more detail."

"When Dr. Marciniak registered for the room next door that you were destined to occupy," Michaelson said to Quentin, "he asked for two keys. He kept one for himself and put the other one in a folder with my name on it. When I checked in for our rooms, the desk clerk gave me your folder and I passed it on to you. The end result was that you and he both had keys to your room."

"Yeah," Quentin said, "but it's your room he ended up in."

"Correct. During his rather passionate discussion with me earlier this afternoon, Dr. Marciniak positioned himself with his back to the adjoining door. By planting his back against the sliding tongue-and-groove lock and shifting position, he was able to unlock this side of that door without being obvious about it. Then, when you and I were safely off to the patio bar, he used the key he'd kept to get into your room. Once there, he unlocked your side of the adjoining door, came through that now completely unlocked door, and went about his business in here."

"If Richard and you hadn't come in prematurely," Marjorie interjected, "Dr. Marciniak would have finished up, relocked the adjoining door, exited through the hallway door, gone back into your room, relocked that side of the adjoining door, and gone back out again. At that point Richard's room would look as if it had been completely locked during the entire time, and there'd be no apparent explanation for anyone without a key getting inside."

"Why go to all that trouble?" Quentin said. "As long as he's registering for rooms, why not just register for yours as well as mine and take the extra key for that one?"

"Registering for mine might have proven a bit awkward," Michaelson said. "If the need arose, Dr. Marciniak wanted the desk clerk to tell the police truthfully that he'd never received a key to my room. That would imply that he'd had no access to it, and that any mischief done here should be laid at someone else's door."

Looking at Marciniak, Marjorie spoke up.

"You really could be forgiven for suggesting to Mr. Quentin at this point that he ought to be able to figure all this out for himself," she said.

Marciniak held his hands up in front of his chest in a gesture of semi-surrender.

"All right already," he said. "I already admitted that you got me. Caught me red-handed searching your room."

"Thanks to Marjorie relocking Quentin's side of the adjoining door," Michaelson said. "Otherwise you would have escaped into his room when you heard the key in my door, and we would have risked chasing each other around like characters in a French farce."

"*That's* why you told me to let the lady into my room while Marciniak was chatting you up," Quentin said. "I thought she was just sort of a lookout."

"Well, I'm duly traumatized," Marciniak said. "It'll probably take me years of therapy to get over this embarrassment. But if you're all through having fun with me, I'll go back to my room and start the therapeutic process with a couple of good, stiff drinks."

"You know," Michaelson said musingly, "it must be going on eighty years since G. K. Chesterton first pointed out that all

American hotels are identical. It's even truer today than when he said it, of course. This Radisson at Hilton Head, to take an example at random, has exactly the same floor plan, layout, color scheme, carpeting, and furniture as the Radisson in Charleston, West Virginia. Everything's the same, right down to the foil-wrapped chocolate mints on the pillows—the same here as in the place where Sharon Bedford was murdered."

"Hold it," Quentin said. "I thought the idea was to smoke this quack out. Where are you going with this Sharon Bedford murdered crap?"

"Dr. Marciniak had exactly the same reason to search Sharon Bedford's room in Charleston as he had to search mine here," Michaelson said. "He used the same key-and-lock trick to get in. As he explained to Wendy Gardner in Charleston, his agency had signed for the oversized end-of-corridor room that some software company was using to demonstrate its products. He registered for that room, took two keys, gave one to the software manager, and kept the other. He had kindly arranged for Ms. Bedford to have the adjoining room."

"Baloney," Marciniak hooted.

"Time-out," Quentin barked, making the fingers-on-palm sign familiar to every football and basketball fan. "That Sunday morning he came into Bedford's room through the hallway door, when she let him in, the same way Pilkington and I did."

"Right," Michaelson said. "That's the way he came in before Ms. Bedford left for breakfast. Early on that Sunday morning, he knocked on her door, came in, and brought his usual intensity to a conversation with her. We'll never know what they talked about, unless Dr. Marciniak chooses to tell us, but I suspect it had something to do with the unconscionability of handing a potentially explosive political document over to you, Mr. Quentin. His emphasizing that point by giving Ms. Bedford one of the praying-for-you-in-heaven cards and explaining its background would explain why the card was in her room."

"Keep it up," Quentin said mordantly. "I'm thick-skinned."

"During this conversation," Michaelson resumed, "Dr. Marciniak surreptitiously unlocked Ms. Bedford's adjoining door, just as he did mine. Then, when she went to breakfast, he used his key to go into the software demonstration room, went through the adjoining door to Ms. Bedford's room, and did successfully there what he tried unsuccessfully to do here."

"Lucky thing for me she went to breakfast," Marciniak said.

"I don't think you left that to chance," Michaelson said. "Her breakfast plans changed immediately after you left her room that morning. Almost as soon as the door had closed behind you, she canceled a room-service Continental breakfast order and went to the café instead. There she ate a breakfast beyond her means, and she used a complimentary meal voucher to pay for it. It's hard to see why she would have been given such a voucher, whereas you, of course, with control over several registrations, would have been given several."

"Now you're guessing," Marciniak said with a shrug. "And what you're guessing at is how I got into her room to search it. I haven't heard anything about murder yet."

"When did you learn she was diabetic?" Michaelson asked.

"I had no idea she was diabetic until I read the autopsy report," Marciniak said.

michael bowen

"Bosh. You used your agency's resources to get your hands on her medical records well before the Charleston conference."

"How can you be sure of that?" Quentin demanded.

"Put it this way," Michaelson answered. "I'm as sure of that as Dr. Marciniak was that Sharon Bedford was a regular smoker."

"Look," Quentin said impatiently, "I do sound bites, okay? Would you please put this shredder-fodder of yours in plain English?"

"The Saturday night of the Charleston conference, Ms. Bedford saw you smoking and asked you for a cigarette so that she could have a few minutes of relative privacy with you while the two of you engaged in that currently unfashionable activity. But she wasn't a habitual smoker, and it showed. A young woman I know named Wendy Gardner noticed instantly that Ms. Bedford's technique was a bit unpracticed. Dr. Marciniak, however, looking at the same scene as Ms. Gardner, seemed morally certain that Ms. Bedford was addicted to tobacco."

"So the fuck what?" Quentin yelped, slapping his thighs with his palms in exasperation.

"You took the words out of my mouth," Marciniak said.

"Dr. Marciniak's misplaced certainty came from his review of Ms. Bedford's medical records. Her blood tests showed nicotine levels consistent with regular consumption of cigarettes. Dr. Marciniak had no way of knowing that that was the accidental result of Ms. Bedford's exposure to heavy doses of secondhand cigarette smoke in the office of the head paralegal at the law firm where she freelanced."

"Riiiight," Quentin said, smiling as if he were trying to

humor a demented half-wit. "And you're telling me about diabetes because—*why*, for God's sake?"

"Because it's the beginning of the answer to the elegant question you asked about her murder," Michaelson said. "I telescoped things a bit in describing Dr. Marciniak's actions that morning. After he left her room the first time, he hung one of the cards asking for early maid service on her door. He didn't make his clandestine entry until after the maid had finished."

"Why?" Marciniak demanded.

"So that you could replace the chocolate mint the maid left on Ms. Bedford's pillow with one laced with toxic bufotenine. Knowing Ms. Bedford was diabetic and that diabetics habitually keep small pieces of candy with them in case they think their blood sugar needs a jolt, you figured she'd certainly take the mint, eat it sometime in the course of the morning—and die. That's what she did."

"I had a *chocolate mint* prepared ahead of time?"

"Of course not. You took the mint from your own pillow, poisoned it, and substituted it for the mint on Ms. Bedford's pillow. Then you relocked the adjoining door and exited through the hallway door, which automatically relocked as it closed. After Ms. Bedford had come back from breakfast, had her chats with Pilkington and Quentin, and was drawing her bath, she ate the mint and poisoned herself. To all appearances, she was killed by something that had to have happened inside her locked room after the maid cleaned it—that is, at a time when you, unlike Pilkington, no longer had apparent access to it."

"You about done now, ace?" Marciniak asked. "I mean, is that it?"

"Almost. The key point, you see, is that you used bufotenine instead of arsenic or strychnine or one of the other
more traditional poisons. I'm told that bufotenine can be absorbed through the tongue and the insides of the lips. Your
original plan included poisoning the filters of her cigarettes as
well as her mint. That's why you were so put out when you
learned you were mistaken in your conjectures about her
smoking habits. Of the three arguable suspects, you're the
only one in a position to have made that mistake. That's why
you have to be the murderer."

"Your whole theory is idiotic," Marciniak said, his voice
now coldly contemptuous. "I had nothing against Sharon Bedford."

"No, you didn't," Michaelson agreed in a tone that matched
Marciniak's chilly contempt with cold anger. "She was just collateral damage. She had to die because you couldn't risk her
giving a duplicate original of the coup d'état order to Quentin
and thereby destroying the value of the one you had."

"And fortunately for me, I happened to be carrying a lethal
dose of bufotenine around just in case I might want to waste
anyone who got in my way."

"You came to the conference thoroughly prepared to murder Sharon Bedford," Michaelson said. "You'd planned the
murder well before either you or she got to Charleston."

"I had no reason to suspect she even had the order until she
started advertising it during the conference," Marciniak said.

"You knew perfectly well that she had the order. Deborah
Moodie told you. She was appalled at the prospect of Quentin
getting the kind of power that that documentation represented. She begged you to keep that from happening by finding Bedford a job with significant political responsibility so
that she wouldn't have to turn to Quentin for one."

"You may not be aware of this," Marciniak said, "but Deborah Moodie isn't one of my biggest fans. She tried to destroy my career, and I ended up having to destroy hers. She'd rather scrub toilets the rest of her life than ask me for anything."

"You're absolutely right about that," Michaelson said, nodding. "Begging a favor from you must have been the hardest thing she ever did. She did it because her country was more important to her than her feelings or her career. But she made that sacrifice in vain."

"Life in the big city, champ. You sound to me like you're making the same mistake she did."

"You recognized the risk that no job you could give Bedford could compete in Bedford's mind with what Quentin could offer her," Michaelson continued. "So you came to Charleston prepared to kill her if you had to. Your fears were realized. She wasn't tempted enough by your offer, so you murdered her."

"I have dedicated my entire life to medicine and the life sciences," Marciniak said. Still the voice was quietly intense, and now a suggestion of smoldering anger had crept into it as well. "I mean since I was fifteen years old. Now, I'm as ambitious as anyone in Washington. I'd pull strings, leak stories, kiss butts, lie, cheat, or steal to get a position I wanted, and I've done all of those things and liked it. But for you to suggest seriously that I would murder a decent and completely innocent human being so that I could add one more title to my résumé is obscene."

"If ambition alone led to murder, the homicide rate for any square block of Constitution Avenue would be higher than for Washington's entire drug corridor," Michaelson said. "You didn't kill Sharon Bedford because you were ambitious. You killed her because you thought you were indispensable. In your own mind, you'd become the only person in America who could save science and medicine from the corrosive, corrupting effect of politics—from the Quentins of the world. That's what made Ms. Bedford's murder a Washington crime. She didn't die because of greed or hatred or lust. She died because of your delusion. She died because you talked yourself into believing your own press releases."

"How much of this can you prove?" Quentin demanded.

Rising, Michaelson walked over to the bed and took the mint from the pillow.

"If this turns out to be laced with bufotenine," he said, "I'd say we can prove a good deal of it."

"Are you saying he'd pull the same thing again?" Quentin asked in astonishment. "Just so he could sell me that piece of paper instead of you?"

"Not primarily," Michaelson said. "I don't think Dr. Marciniak will give the document to you except as a last resort. But he didn't just sneak in here to search my room. He also came in to kill me under circumstances that would permanently compromise you, Mr. Quentin."

"What do you mean?"

"Oh, come now," Michaelson scoffed. "This is your field. Two people at two separate hotels who have something you want die under mysterious circumstances while you're in the neighborhood. That would be the Vince Foster suicide mess squared, wouldn't it? Do you really think you'd keep on breezing into the Oval Office with three bright ideas a day after something like that hit the papers?"

"But Marciniak would've been as compromised as I would have," Quentin protested.

"I think not," Michaelson said. "On the contrary, I think he'd feed the leaks and eventually posture himself as a sort of detective-scientist, fearlessly exposing the truth."

Caught up in this exchange, Michaelson, Marjorie, and Quentin were all unprepared when Marciniak leaped forward. Quentin reacted first, tensing and crouching slightly to block the doorway.

But Marciniak wasn't headed for the door. In three quick strides he reached Michaelson, who looked around just in time to catch Marciniak's left forearm smashing across his face.

Dazed, Michaelson staggered backward against a window and slumped toward the floor, barely catching himself on the wide sill. He clenched his fist reflexively around the mint, but his strength didn't approach Marciniak's. In less than a second Marciniak held the foil-wrapped candy.

Marjorie was hustling desperately toward Marciniak. A whiplike backhand sent her reeling. As she stumbled to all fours, Marciniak popped the mint into his mouth and swallowed it.

Giving his throbbing head two hard shakes, Michaelson cleared the red-and-black fog stealing over his eyes. He saw his assailant sagging on the floor a yard or so away. Marciniak sank to a seated position with his back braced against the wall. His head cocked toward his right shoulder, tongue lolling from his open mouth.

Squatting beside the man, Michaelson grasped Marciniak's chin and moved it a couple of inches. No resistance, no reaction. Foamy pink drool bubbled from the right corner of his mouth.

"Go downstairs to the front desk and tell them to get help

up here," Michaelson said over his shoulder to Quentin, who was still frozen by the door.

As Quentin moved to obey, Michaelson began to feel Marciniak's pockets urgently. Dabbing at blood that pooled along her lower lip, Marjorie worked her way over to Michaelson.

"I haven't been hit that hard since before my divorce," Marjorie said. "Should I call nine-one-one? They might get an emergency crew here faster than the hotel will."

"It's academic," Michaelson muttered. "I wanted Quentin out of the way, but even if they could get a tube down Marciniak's throat in the next thirty seconds, it wouldn't make the slightest difference."

Michaelson pulled two key-cards from Marciniak's shirt pocket and held them out to Marjorie.

"One of these should open six-fifteen," he said. "You know what to look for."

"If removing it is probably a serious crime, I do," she said, taking the keys. "If the police look like they're on their way up, give me a ring, will you?"

"Count on it."

Marjorie bolted for the door. Feeling a spasm of weakness in his knees, Michaelson stood up and leaned once more against the windowsill. Perhaps ten seconds later he heard an amplified voice barking over an intercom.

"May we have your attention. Is there a doctor in the hotel? If there is a doctor in the hotel, please contact the front desk immediately from any phone."

After a pause, the message was repeated. As he heard the voice ask for the second time, "Is there a doctor in the hotel?" Michaelson unconsciously shook his head. Not anymore there wasn't.

In efficient but unhurried silence a white-jacketed waiter cleared heavy china plates and crystal stemware away from the four places at a table set in the middle of the ceremonial reception room on the eighth floor of the State Department. A second waiter slid substantial glass ashtrays and bulbous snifters into place on the rich linen tablecloth. Reappearing, the first waiter filled each of the snifters with Courvoisier.

"Success," Pilkington said, smiling and raising his glass as the waiters withdrew.

Michaelson, Marjorie, and Quentin raised their glasses in polite response and joined Pilkington in a fastidious, throat-scorching sip. Marciniak's suicide lay six days in the past. Quentin's minions had searched thoroughly for Marciniak's duplicate of the coup d'état order but hadn't found it. The Washington media were all over the suicide, but seemed inclined so far to be buying the spin that Quentin had thoughtfully put on it.

"You know," Quentin said contentedly, "in the last forty-eight hours I've actually started to believe that it's going to work. We're going to bring this off. All of us."

He glanced down to his right and behind him in case anyone at the table had missed the significance of the last three words. One of the several important chambers on the seventh floor, immediately below them, was the Office of the Secretary-designate. That was where an incoming secretary of state sat during the transition, before he (no shes so far) had been sworn in, while he waited for his predecessor to wrap things up and clear out.

Michaelson reached beneath his chair and brought up a wooden cigar box, roughly twice the size of the cardboard variety. A rich-smelling gasp of air escaped as he opened the lid.

"These are quite legal, by the way," he said as he offered the open box to Marjorie. "Hand rolled in this country by individual craftsmen under the supervision of Miguel de Santiago."

"No, thank you," Marjorie said, waving the proffered box away. "I smoked a cigar about twenty years ago, and if I have another one so soon, I might develop an unhealthy taste for them."

Michaelson shifted the box to Pilkington, who with an expression suggesting vast appreciation and a questioning raise of his eyebrows lifted one of the three cigars in the box.

"By all means," Michaelson murmured, smiling.

Pilkington held the Havana before him in the fingertips of both hands as he examined it with a connoisseur's relish. Taking the penultimate cigar for himself, Michaelson shifted the box across the table to offer it to Quentin. Had Quentin been paying attention, he might have realized that the box must have held only three cigars to start with, which would have left them one short had Marjorie not demurred. But he wasn't paying attention.

After they had completed the lighting ritual, the three men sat back with Marjorie in smoky blue complacency and re-hashed the improbable sequence of events that had led to and then followed from Sharon Bedford's murder. Oversized though they were, the cigars burned inexorably lower as the brandy snifters emptied and coffee cups replaced them. For years afterward Michaelson would remember with sea-sun sharpness the textured mellowness of that twenty-five-minute period and the sense of uncomplicated contentment that seemed to suffuse Quentin during it.

"Your key break in this thing," Quentin said to Michaelson toward the end. "Did you get the critical information legiti-mately or corruptly? Was it volunteered or procured?"

"I'll answer your questions in order," Michaelson said, thinking of his talk with Quentin in the Old Executive Office Building. "Corruptly. Procured."

"Now," Quentin said as he ground out a cigar stub less than an inch long, "enough about the past. Let's talk about the future."

"Hear hear," Pilkington said quietly.

"I know you don't think I'm much of a gentleman," Quen-tin said to Michaelson, "but I'm gentleman enough to enjoy a good cigar, and I keep my word. More important, I know you're a gentleman. I know that tonight you're going to keep your promise to give me Bedford's hard copy of the coup d'état order. And I know this won't be the last celebratory dinner the four of us have."

"There are three more things you should know," Pilking-ton said, smiling primly. "First, you are no gentleman. Sec-ond, you wouldn't know a good cigar if you had one shoved up your nose."

"And third," Michaelson said as Quentin's mouth gaped a

bit, "I've already kept my promise. I gave you Ms. Bedford's duplicate of the coup d'état order, and I gave it to you tonight."

"What do you mean?" Quentin managed.

"Your cigar was wrapped in it. You've spent the last half-hour smoking it."

"But—but *why*?" Quentin sputtered.

"It's like jazz," Michaelson said. "If you don't understand, I can't explain it to you."

"You total moron," Quentin spat. "And you fucking cretin on top of it. You had it in the palm of your hand."

"I know."

"What do you think? Do you seriously believe that silly little task force of yours is going anywhere? Do you think it's getting a penny's worth of funding after nine A.M. tomorrow?"

"No."

"You threw away the last chance you'll ever have just so this patronizing, Ivy League fossil across the table from me will smile at you and pat you on the head and tell you how you did the old school proud. You've just fucked yourself—big time and permanently. You'll never be a player again. As of this moment and for the rest of your meaningless fucking life, you're even more irrelevant than you have been up to now."

"Politics is fickle." Michaelson shrugged. "I think Sharon Bedford and Deborah Moodie would have approved of the choice I made. That's more important to me than your good opinion."

"You may be excused, Mr. Quentin," Pilkington interjected then. "Please take with you as you leave the sincere hope of everyone at the department that you enjoy the remainder of your stay in Washington."

Tight-lipped, Quentin rose stiffly from the table and stalked from the room.

"Up in smoke," Pilkington said then. "With Marciniak's copy apparently unrecoverable, we just destroyed the last documentary evidence of an act of treason. Quite bracing, actually. A crime dwarfing Watergate and everything since. Except for presidential assassinations and secession, maybe the greatest political crime in the nation's history. And we've just covered it up."

"For a political crime, though," Michaelson said, "it had a certain grandeur about it. It wasn't venal or self-interested. It wasn't some tawdry vote-fiddle like Watergate or a money-grab like Teapot Dome and Whitewater. They were trying to save the country."

"And that makes it okay?" Pilkington demanded sharply.

"Certainly not. The most you can say for it is that it might not have been entirely misguided. However you might defend the order, though, it represented a failure of confidence in the Constitution and the country itself."

"Which strikes me as less than commendable," Pilkington said.

"Me, too," Michaelson said. "It's an apt topic for a scholarly debate or a word in the ear of someone choosing running mates or cabinet members or even a congressional hearing someday. But it doesn't strike me as an appropriate instrument for job-seeking purposes—or as a very promising subject for a series of thirty-second campaign ads designed by the likes of Mr. Quentin."

"Speaking of whom," Pilkington said then pensively, "it's tempting to give your Southern friend Mr. Gallagher the full story about Quentin's role in this affair. He might do the little fellow considerable physical violence."

Michaelson shook his head, frowning with distaste.

"That would be like using a Shefield steel saber to trim a Tiparillo," he said. "Marjorie and I and Johnny Walker Black met for some time last night with Todd Gallagher. He now knows how Sharon Bedford was murdered and how much he did to bring the facts to light. More important, he understands that she died for something that mattered, at least to her—that she wasn't just collateral damage. I intend for him to go on understanding that."

"No doubt you're right," Pilkington said dismissively. "However that may be, and for what it's worth, I deeply appreciate what both of you have done."

"Thank you," Marjorie said as she glanced at the door through which Quentin had exited, "but we didn't actually do it for you."

"I know you didn't," Pilkington said. "I suppose I'd be a little disappointed in you if you had."

"Careful," Michaelson said. "A little self-knowledge is a dangerous thing. And neither of us is buying it anyway."

"Fair enough," Pilkington said. "Enough fencing. Once and for all, before we adjourn: Did you or did you not find Marciniak's copy of the order? I really do have to know."

He looked searchingly at Marjorie. An expert scrutinizing her bland expression couldn't have said whether she was holding a royal flush or a pair of deuces. He shifted his gaze to Michaelson.

"Define 'know,' " Michaelson said.